IN WANT OF A WIFE

A PEMBERLEY RANCH ROMANCE BOOK 1

SHANAE JOHNSON

THOSE JOHNSON GIRLS

CHAPTER ONE

"I think he's going to propose." The words spoken by the redhead were dreamy. Her strawberry blonde curls softly framed her face in delicate, cheery wisps, like a lover's kiss. Her green eyes were as wide as a doe's filled with hope and anticipation.

"Are you out of your mind?" The second redhead glared. Her bone straight red hair was more the color of an apple than a strawberry. A classic red that was vibrant and deep. The color that most imagined when someone thought of a redhead. The eyes were the exact same shade of green. Instead of eagerness, her brow quirked with incredulity. "We only went on two dates. And I didn't even realize the first one was actually a date until it was over."

"The third date is dinner with the family," the third redhead of the bunch said. Her pixie cut locks were of the darkest shade of red; the color auburn. A shade that touched the color brown but was far from mousy. "You know what that means."

Charlotte Lee caught sight of her own reflection in the kitchen window. It was easy to catch sight of herself. She was the mousey brown-haired girl in the bunch of tall, statuesque, vibrant redheads with porcelain skin. Charlotte's tanned skin wasn't a product of the sun, rather a gift from her father, who'd brought it over with him from Shanghai as a college student.

"This isn't a date," said the classic red. Eliza Bennett rolled her eyes as she towered over the top of her sisters' heads. The eye roll was meant solely for Charlotte, as though her best friend was the only one who understood her. "Will you tell them, Charlie?"

Charlotte didn't bother answering her friend. She knew the edict was entirely rhetorical. Not a full second later, Eliza proved that by providing a statement in answer to her own question.

"What man in his right mind would ask a woman who is clearly trying to ghost him to marry him?"

Fair point, Charlotte thought to herself. She also

wondered if Eliza was still being rhetorical since she answered her question with a question? Was that, instead, ironic?

English hadn't been Charlotte's strong point in school. Her strengths had come in the after-school animal husbandry program, where she'd spent time with the other kids whose parents worked long hours.

Charlotte's parents didn't work long hours. Or at least she supposed they didn't. She couldn't imagine that souls had to work in heaven. Back here on earth, Charlotte had stayed after school learning to work with farm animals because it was better being there than in her aunt's home and constantly being in the way. Or being reminded that she was an unwanted and unwelcome burden.

"Collin invited himself over to talk business with Dad," Eliza said as though that was the end of the conversation.

The girls peered around the corner of the kitchen that led into the dining area. There, a barrel-chested John Bennett sat across from a tall and lanky Collin Hunsford. Mr. Bennett sipped at his coffee, thumbing through the day's newspaper. Collin looked out the window toward where the Bennetts's prized race horse grazed his evening meal. Neither man had spoken a word since Collin had come to the door.

Collin looked up just then. In a choreographed move, the three Bennett sisters pirouetted, turning away from the corner and leaping out of sight. Charlotte missed the beat and was left standing on stage under the glaring spotlight of Collin's piercing blue gaze.

Charlotte had had two left feet all her life. There was no way she could twirl away without falling down flat. She couldn't have lifted up onto her tippy toes if she'd tried because the heels of her worn, hand-me-down cowboy boots were rooted to the ground. So there she stood, caught in Collin's gaze.

Collin Hunsford had that type of gaze that stripped away all of the fluff and saw right to the heart of the matter. Unlike all the other guys she'd grown up with, Collin didn't shout others down to be heard. He only spoke if spoken to and only responded when he knew the answer. Otherwise, his attention was wholly and entirely devoted to the animals in his care.

Charlotte had spent a fair amount of her time in the after-school program studying him to know that fact about him. Though Collin never spared her a second glance. Most boys didn't.

Even now, his gaze slipped past her. Searching out Eliza, no doubt. Which is exactly as it should be. Since the man was courting her best friend's favor.

Charlotte should probably get out of the way so that he could see better. Before she could do the courtesy of moving aside, Collin turned his attention back to the window. His gaze on the horse grazing outside.

Maybe Jane and Lydia were wrong? Maybe Collin wasn't here to propose to Eliza? What man proposed after two dates outside of a romance novel?

Collin appeared far more interested in Lefroy. The Bennetts's prize-winning stallion had been having some trouble with his joints of late. Charlotte had noticed his gait was off when she'd ridden him earlier. It's something she would've told his trainer, Bert. Except they had sent Bert off with a grand retirement this past weekend. The lights were out at the little cottage at the edge of the property. It sat empty, waiting for Mr. Bennett to make a decision about its new occupant.

"Whatever he's doing here has nothing to do with me," Eliza was saying.

"Oh?" said Lydia. "Then why does he have a bulge in his side pocket?"

Three red heads whipped back around the corner in search of evidence. Charlotte had already pulled away, out of step once more. She didn't need a second glance at Collin. She'd already caught one glimpse and could recall every detail of the man.

The man was tall and lean. He had classic features that would make him handsome if he ever smiled. Which he rarely did. Not that she was counting his smiles. Or his frowns.

There was a quiet intensity to Collin Hunsford that often called Charlotte's eyes to him. So it was no wonder that she had seen a definite bulge in his pants pocket when he'd arrived for family dinner with the Bennetts.

"Trust me," said Eliza. "It's not what you think it is."

"I thought it was a man's feet that told you about...you know," said Lydia.

"Lydia," admonished Jane, her cheeks pinkening.

"No," said Eliza. "I think it's actually the nose."

"Eliza," huffed Jane, her cheeks now a full-on red blush.

Eliza and Lydia threw their heads back and laughed, their own cheeks turning red with the effort. Charlotte couldn't hide the giggle that rose in her throat. Jane was the Bennet sister who was always easy to rile up with her proper manners.

It was at times like these where Charlotte loved that she had been welcomed into the Bennett family. This house had always been a warm and welcoming haven. The complete opposite to her aunt's cold apartment where Charlotte had had to sit still, be quiet, and know her place. Here at the Bennett Ranch, Charlotte had learned to run, she'd learned to shout, she'd learned to ride.

Mr. Bennett had never said no when Eliza asked if Charlotte could spend the night. But in the morning, after a hearty breakfast of banana pancakes, he'd load Charlotte up in his truck and take her back to her aunt's where Charlotte would count the days, the hours, the minutes until the weekend would return and she could return to stay another night.

And now, with Bert retired, Charlotte was hoping she could go into that old cottage and have a place to stay, a place of her own, surrounded by her favorite people in the world. But to do that, she had to convince Mr. Bennett that she—a recent community college graduate with only volunteer experience and an internship—was the best candidate for horse trainer.

"Eliza, dear, you're being rude to your guest,"

called Mr. Bennet. The older man caught Charlotte's gaze from the dining room. He grinned as though she were in on some joke. Charlotte grinned back.

As a little girl, she'd secretly dreamed that Mr. Bennett would adopt her and bring her to live here at their ranch. She certainly spent enough time here after Eliza had decided they would be friends. But Charlotte supposed the widower had his hands full with three rambunctious girls of his own. He couldn't handle another.

Charlotte was no longer a little orphan with her hand out. She was a grown woman with a degree and qualifications. She had her fingers and toes crossed that nepotism would be on her side when she made her pitch for the trainer job.

"I'm helping Jane with dinner," called Eliza from the opposite side of the kitchen from the stove where she was ardently helping the wall stand tall by leaning against it. "And he's not my guest. We broke up."

That last bit was said under her breath, only loud enough for the women gathered in the kitchen to hear it.

"Does he know that, Eliza?" asked Jane, pulling a fragrant roast surrounded by potatoes and squash from the oven.

"He should since I haven't been returning his texts or calls all week." Eliza kicked off the wall, following the scent of the dish.

One by one, the girls filed out of the kitchen. Lydia behind Jane, who took a seat at the far end of the table. Charlotte followed behind Eliza, bringing up the rear. When she entered the dining room, there were only two seats left. One diagonally across from Collin. The other right beside him.

It was no wonder that Eliza dashed off to the other side of the table, and Charlotte wound up sitting right next to Collin. Once again, he didn't spare her a glance as she sat down. He stood when the four women entered the room. Four pairs of eyes zeroed in on the man's front pocket. There was a definite bulge in there.

"You look well tonight, Elizabeth," said Collin. "Very healthy."

"Thank you," said Eliza stiffly.

"There's something I wanted to talk with you about," Collin began. "Do you think we could—"

"Is it about The Pemberley Races?" said Eliza. "I hear Darcy is bringing in some big television star as a draw. Did you hear that, Dad?"

Mr. Bennett didn't look up from carving the roast. "No, can't say that I have."

"Any idea who that might be?" asked Lydia, her gaze on Collin as she twirled a dark tendril of hair.

"Uh, no," said Collin, who was still standing. He ran his hands down his pants, passing over the bulge in his side pocket. "As I was saying, Eliza—"

"I'll bet it's Carlos Bingley, the star of that Telenovela," said Lydia. "What's it called again, Jane?"

"Ummm, I can't remember." Jane's gaze was fixated on the hump of something that was slowly creeping up the lining of Collin's pocket.

"Elizabeth, it's really important that I speak with you privately."

"There's nothing you can have to say to me that you can't say in front of my family."

Collin looked at each Bennett in turn. He didn't spare a glance for Charlotte. Which she supposed was fine, as she wasn't officially a part of this family. Even though she'd been invited by Eliza, who had been calling and texting her all week as per usual of best friends.

Eliza slid Charlotte a wary glance, rolling her eyes as she cut into her helping of roast. Eliza often rolled her eyes due to the world misunderstanding her. She explained to Charlotte that being misunderstood was the plight of the middle child. Charlotte had not understood the sentiment when Eliza always spoke loudly and clearly of her beliefs and her demands.

"So be it." Collin nodded.

He reached into his pants pocket. Everyone held their breath… and then let out a collective yelp when he pulled out what looked like a weapon. But, being that they had all grown up on a ranch, they each knew it was a horse twitch.

"Told you," said Eliza, raising her brow.

Collin wasn't done emptying his pockets. Next, he brought out a ring box. The next sound around the table was complete and utter silence.

CHAPTER TWO

Collin reached in his pocket for the ring box. Instead of the velvet box left to him by his mother, his fingers wrapped around cold steel. The horse twitch pinched his index finger as he grabbed hold of it and laid it on the dining room table.

He'd come over to the Bennett's after working on one of his cousin Darcy's prized stallions. That Thoroughbred had needed first an x-ray, followed by joint injections. Because Collin hadn't wanted to sedate the racing horse with drugs that could disqualify him for his next race, he'd used the twitch. The restraining device might look like a tool of torture, but in truth, when it was used correctly, it hit on a pressure point that released soothing endorphins and affected calm in a horse. Collin had managed to take his films and medicate the horse in record time, keeping all parties out of harm's way.

Looking down at the twitch, Collin wondered if it might be of use here at the Bennett Ranch. He didn't like the stuttering steps of their prized race horse, Lefroy. He should go out and take a closer look.

But not until after.

He'd come here with a purpose. Best to get it done first. He'd learned that women did not like it when he put horses before them.

With that thought, Collin reached back into his pocket and pulled out the velvet case. In it was the Chanel Set engagement ring his mother had left him. Collin had always liked the alignment of the diamonds on the side of the band. The large one at the center sparkled whenever his mother was out in the sunlight, which hadn't been often.

Eliza Bennett spent her days out in the sun, whether rain or shine. That would be a boon of this union; he'd get to see the band twinkle when she became his wife.

"Elizabeth," he began, as he hated the nickname

Eliza. He'd never understood the need to truncate or change names. "I would like to offer you my hand as a partner in life."

The box opened with a pop. The diamonds sparkled under the overhead light. Collin noted that the entire room fell quiet. He'd have to remember this trick at future family gatherings. Present a jewelry box, and the room would turn blessedly silent.

Lost in that silence was Elizabeth's response. She hadn't said yes yet.

Collin was uncertain if he should say more? Or if he should let the silence reign on. He was in favor of the silence.

Whenever he encountered Elizabeth with her family or friends, she was always vociferous. The woman had lots to say, and she said it loudly. That was the one drawback of choosing Elizabeth to be his life partner. Her family was often loud and frenetic. It grated on Collin's nerves with so much activity. Yet, whenever they were alone together, she quieted, which raised his estimation of her.

"You can't be serious." Elizabeth's voice boomed into the quiet.

Her volume caused Collin to flinch. Outside,

Lefroy whinnied and cantered a couple of steps away. His ears twitched, trying to pinpoint the sound. Like all prey animals, horses had very sensitive hearing.

Collin's ears twitched as he looked around at those gathered at the table. He looked first to Mr. Bennett, who had been reading the evening paper since Collin sat down at the table. The man's facial expression was unchanged, as though he was still reading the paper. Only now, his eyes scanned back and forth between Collin and his daughter, as though he was reading the story unfolding in his dining room. There was no smile or frown to indicate enjoyment or displeasure. Just a flat line.

That didn't help Collin at all. He'd studied facial expressions as a teen. Not by choice. His mother and aunt had made him so that he could be more sociable. Their ploy to make Collin more companionable didn't work. But he'd learned some valuable lessons. The main one being that there were nineteen different kinds of smiles that could be categorized, quantified, and identified.

Both Jane and Lydia had their lips pressed together in the approximation of a smile. But the corners of their mouths didn't get very high. Neither smile reached their eyes.

Jane Bennett's smile was one of embarrassment, as noted by her flushed cheeks and the way her head tilted slightly downward and to the left. Lydia Bennet also had a downward tilt to her head, but her cheeks were raised and puffed out, displaying the telltale signs of a dampening smile. A dampening smile was a smile that said the individual knew they shouldn't be smiling, but it was the only way they could keep from laughing.

Collin froze as he waited for it. His entire body shut down as he stood towering over every person at the Bennett's dining room table. He felt like a small child unable to get away from it. His stomach muscles twitched, preparing to twist into knots the second it happened.

Only it didn't. No one was laughing at him. Not a single finger pointed at him, poked at him to show that he was different from everybody else. Wrong in some way that no one could quantify.

Collin's gaze landed on the last person at the table. Charlotte Lee had sat down beside him moments ago without a word. He had assumed Elizabeth would sit beside him, but he'd been relieved when Charlotte took the seat. She was as quiet as a mouse growing up. Now that she was full-grown, she had kept that characteristic.

She gazed up at him. Her lips sealed, her brows furrowed. She wasn't laughing at him. She looked concerned. Her posture indicated that she was somewhat uncomfortable. As though some social faux pas had been committed.

But what could it be? He'd followed the script to the letter. He'd taken Elizabeth out on two dates to indicate his interest in pursuing a partnership with her. He knew that on the third date was when a commitment was expected, and here he was with a ring.

What was he missing?

He looked to Charlotte again. He'd always been able to read her expressions growing up. Unlike other girls, her feelings were written clearly on her face.

Charlotte smiled at him this time. Her smile reached her eyes. But the message she conveyed was not one of happiness or congratulations. The smile was fleeting. It dropped a second later as though it was too heavy for her to hold. And that's when Collin realized his mistake.

He strode over to Elizabeth's side of the table. Once there, he lowered himself to his knee. "My apologies," he said. "I'll start again."

"Don't." Elizabeth held up her hands as though to ward him off. "I'm not marrying you."

"Have I missed some other social cue?" Collin looked over his shoulder to Charlotte again. She was staring at her hands. Meanwhile, all the Bennetts stared at him. The smiles dropped from their faces as they peered at the scene.

"What makes you think I would marry you?" Elizabeth was saying.

Collin turned his attention back to his bride-to-be. He needed her cooperation in this matter in order to achieve his goal. "You gave me the signs."

"Signs? What signs?"

When a mare was in season, she announced by making sure all the stallions knew she was prime for breeding. The signs she gave off were crystal clear. She'd flip her tail up and urinate to get the male horses' attention. Elizabeth was constantly flipping her hair when she spoke in a crowd.

Collin didn't say any of that. He had learned females—human women—didn't appreciate being compared to horses. Just as much as they disliked when he put the horses before them.

Collin rested his outstretched hand with the ring box on his knee. "I heard you say that everybody knows a single guy with a good job must want to be in a committed relationship."

"When did I say that?"

"When you were registering Lefroy for the annual Pemberley Races at my cousin Darcy's ranch."

"Oh." A frown creased Elizabeth's forehead. "I was talking about Darcy. All those over-frilled sweethearts were fawning all over him like he was the second coming."

Like with smiles, Collin had always had trouble with sarcasm. Unfortunately, there was no measurable way to determine irony unless someone laughed after the statement. He couldn't remember if Elizabeth had laughed? But that wasn't the only signal.

"When we went out on our dates, you kept going to the bathroom."

Elizabeth's brows scrunched together in the universal look of confusion.

"Mares urinate to announce they're ready to breed."

Elizabeth balked. "I went to the bathroom to get a break from you."

Jane winced and took in a sharp intake of air.

Lydia snorted and clapped her hands together in

one loud, booming crack.

Collin looked to Charlotte again. Her expression was pained. Her gaze darted to the door as though she desperately wanted to be on the other side of it. He probably shouldn't have made an analogy to Elizabeth and a mare in heat. At least he hadn't gone into the part about how mares flipped their tales to make their intentions crystal clear to a stallion. Not that Elizabeth had done that.

But that wasn't the only reason he'd chosen her. "We're neighbors, so there would be no need for you to move far."

"I live next to Darcy on the other side. You don't see me throwing myself at him."

"You and my cousin do not get on. Whereas we tolerate each other's company quite well." Collin thought back to all the silences they shared on their two dates. She hadn't pressed him for much conversation at all. In fact, he couldn't remember any conversation between the two of them.

"Tolerate? Do you think that's what love is?"

"I don't see where love comes into the equation? I chose you because we wouldn't interrupt each other's life much. We could go on as we are now. Such an alliance will suit everyone involved."

"An alliance? You talk about marriage as though it's a business transaction."

That's exactly what it was. His mother's marriage to his father had solidified the land holdings of Rosings Ranch. Now Collin needed the inheritance money his mother left him to turn the ranch into a haven for retired race horses. But he wouldn't gain access to that money until he put this ring on a woman's finger.

"Technically, that's exactly what marriage is," he said. "It's a contract, historically an alliance between families. The ploy of love and marrying for it is an entirely modern concept that has a very low success rate. Whereas unions based on economic matters are far more successful."

The chorus of intakes of breaths was another clue that he'd gotten it wrong. Every single Bennett was frowning at him. Elizabeth's hands were clenched into tight fists. Jane shook her head slowly from side to side, in the clear language of disappointment. Lydia's nose wrinkled as though she smelled something foul.

Collin looked again to Charlotte. Her face was a mask that was entirely closed off. For once, her expression was completely unreadable to him.

"That's enough, son." That quiet voice came from

the head of the table. Mr. Bennett's expression was still a blank line, but his words made his feelings clear. "I think it's time you leave."

Collin rose up from bended knee. He stuffed the ring box into his pocket and grabbed the twitch from the table. Though he was still confused about his error, he did as he was told and walked to the door, knowing that his aunt would not be pleased with this poor social performance.

CHAPTER THREE

"Can you believe that just happened?"

Someone had once told Charlotte that when a friend wanted a heart to heart, they always went to the friend who would give them the advice they wanted to hear. Charlotte knew what Eliza wanted to hear.

"I know, right," said Charlotte.

"I mean, Collin Hunsford could never make me happy. And I'm sure I'm the last woman in the world who would make him happy."

Eliza paced the length of her bedroom. She reached the window, about-faced, and then walked to the door, where she about-faced again. With each turn, her mane of hair flipped over her shoulder, like a mare warding off the advances of an eager stallion.

"Yeah, I know," said Charlotte from her perch on Eliza's pink bedspread. Much of the room was done up in shades of pink, which should've been a contrast to her non-frilly friend. When Eliza had heard that redheads should never wear pink, she doubled down, as was her personality.

"He thought I was giving him signs? I barely remembered to put on lip gloss on that second date."

"Hmmm, I know."

Outside the bedroom window, Lefroy shifted his weight from one leg to another. Charlotte did not like the way he was standing. The next couple of steps he took were normal, and his gait appeared to level out. Maybe she was imagining things? The only way to be sure would be to take him to a vet. Too bad the best vet in town just got rejected while the roast was being served.

"That was completely unreal. I wonder if it was a bet? Maybe Darcy put him up to it?"

"Yeah, I know."

"You do?"

The stomping across the hardwoods came to a stop. In the silence, Charlotte turned from the window. "I do what?"

"Know that Darcy made a bet with Collin to propose?" Eliza plopped down on the bed beside Charlotte.

And now they were on Eliza's favorite topic of all-time; pin the blame on Fitz Darcy. The cold war between the two had been going on for as long as Charlotte could remember. She had no idea how it began.

"That doesn't sound like Darcy," said Charlotte.

"How would you know? Have you spoken to him?"

"I thought we were talking about Collin?"

"We were. We are." Eliza stood and resumed her pacing. "I couldn't care what Darcy would have to say."

"I know."

"Exactly," said Eliza.

Charlotte had lost the thread of the conversation. She wasn't sure if they were talking about Darcy or Collin right now. In either case, the response was the same.

"I know," Charlotte piped in obediently.

"He really thought I'd say yes to that monstrosity of a proposal."

Oh, they were back on Collin. Although Charlotte hadn't thought his proposal was entirely out of bounds. When she picked his words apart, it made sense. No, it was not at all romantic as Eliza would have wanted. But not every girl got romance.

Collin had offered Eliza what Charlotte prized most in the world; a home of her own. But even better, a home on a ranch filled with horses and wide-open spaces. Charlotte knew Collin was turning Rosings Ranch into a haven for retired race horses. But it wasn't just horses there. As a veterinarian, Collin took in any animal that needed a healing touch. Living at Rosings sounded like heaven to Charlotte.

Not that he'd ever dream of proposing to her. Charlotte didn't ever expect a man to go down on one knee for her. Which was fine. She would be the one doing the proposing for the job and the security that she craved.

"Is it so wrong of me to want passion and excitement in a relationship?" said Eliza.

"No, I think you should have that if it's what you want."

"It's what we both deserve. We're attractive, intelligent, capable women. We need men to match that."

Charlotte knew what she was expected to say. But the two words *I know* wouldn't make it past her throat. Not a single boy or man in this town had ever looked twice at her.

"That was so bizarre," Eliza went on. "He couldn't have been serious. I'm still leaning toward a bet with Darcy. They're probably laughing about it right now over at Pemberley."

Charlotte didn't think Collin was laughing. She'd seen the confusion and embarrassment on his face at Eliza's rejection. The man had been serious. Though Charlotte couldn't understand why he had chosen Eliza.

No, strike that. Charlotte knew exactly why any man would choose Eliza. Eliza was all the things she'd said the two of them were. She was the prettiest girl in town—only outshined by her older sister Jane who was ethereal in her beauty. But Eliza was smarter, wittier.

And Charlotte loved her friend for all those reasons. Though Charlotte had never understood why Eliza had chosen her as her closest confidante? Maybe it was because Charlotte was her exact opposite? She'd never asked. She wasn't sure she actually wanted to know the answer. Charlotte was simply happy to be included.

"We'll see Darcy tomorrow when we take Lefroy in for his pre-race exam," Charlotte said.

Eliza rolled her eyes and flipped her hair over her shoulder. It was a move Charlotte had seen mares do when they wanted to attract a particular stallion's attention. Hmmm? Maybe Collin had gotten that signal right. It just hadn't been meant for him.

"Speaking of the Pemberley Races," Charlotte went on, "I wanted to talk with your dad about the trainer position."

"Oh, wait until you meet the new trainer, Charlie."

"New… trainer?"

"You're going to love her. Yes! He hired a woman, which is so twenty-first century of him. She'll be moving into the cabin next week in time for the races."

Charlotte had to clear her throat and tamp down her disappointment. She hadn't even had the chance to apply, and now her plan was unraveling. She looked out the window toward the cabin.

The sun was starting to set, but the rays touched down on the structure. For the first time, Charlotte noted that the roof was missing a few shingles. The paint on the side was dull. There were patches of dirt amidst the blades of grass. Still, it looked better to her than the cold apartment that had been her home for the last two decades.

"I'm gonna go grab a tub of ice cream," Eliza was saying. "Lord knows I need it after that proposal debacle. You spending the night?"

Disappointment still clogged her throat. So Charlotte nodded her head. She'd spend the night tonight. But just like always, in the morning, someone would drive her back to her aunt's, where she'd be cooped up inside a cold, quiet, cramped space where she had always been unwanted.

Charlotte looked to the outside again. Not to the trainer's cabin this time. She looked to the pen that housed Lefroy, the horse she'd learned to ride on.

"I'm gonna take Lefroy out for a quick ride first."

CHAPTER FOUR

Collin gathered his horse's reins in his hands. The move signaled to the stallion that something was about to happen. Something was about to happen, something both man and beast needed. To run far and fast.

Lifting up a little on his grounding strap, Collin squeezed his calves into Equus's side. The horse immediately got the message of Collin's signal. It picked up its pace, and they were off.

The wind whipped Collin's hair. The fresh air sailed into his nostrils, helping to clear his mind. Only one thought intruded, and it was a welcome thought. Collin wished all creatures could communicate as clearly as a man and his horse.

Collin wanted to ride this fast forever. But

horses weren't machines. They could only maintain this pace for a few miles. And so he signaled Equus to slow. Unfortunately, as the horse came down from a full-on run to a slower jog, Collin's thoughts walked back into his head.

He'd been so close to meeting the demands of his Aunt Catherine. But now, with Eliza's rejection of his well-logicked proposal, he was back at square one.

Collin hated playing games. He was most uncomfortable with games of chance, especially when his life and the lives of other animals that depended on him were in the balance.

Unfortunately, the only way to balance his books and move forward with his plans for his ranch was to get his hands on his inheritance. The same inheritance that came with the condition that he be married before the strings his mother had attached to the purse be cut. Even from the grave, his mother was still trying to get her socially awkward son to make friends. As a child, and now as a man, the only people who Collin could make small talk with all had four legs and only a little grasp of the English language.

Though when Equus, one of the most well-trained horses Collin had in his stables, reared,

Collin couldn't understand why. Until he saw Lefroy do the same as they all rounded a bend.

Collin managed to keep his seat. Whichever Bennett had been riding Lefroy hadn't faired so well.

Great. This was likely going in the unfriendly rejection column the Bennetts had begun tallying this night. At least he knew that social custom insisted he make his way over to the person before tending to the horse.

When Collin dismounted and made his way to the person on the ground, he saw womanly curves. He didn't see any red hair. Instead, hair the color of rich soil lay curled around blades of grass.

"Charlotte?"

Charlotte Lee pushed at the ground until she was sitting upright. When she did so, she winced.

Collin dropped to his knees. In his training, he knew he first had to check the cardiovascular network. And so he put his ear to Charlotte's chest.

"Hey." Charlotte slapped at the side of his head. "What do you think you're doing?"

"Checking your heart."

She stilled, her body going completely rigid. The thump of her chest against the side of his face increased, nearly catching up to the speed at which

Equus had run only moments ago. Charlotte was hearty and hale.

Collin knew he had to check for breaks next. He reached down to her right ankle. Using gentle pressure, he began to search for any sign of pain. When he got to her knee, Charlotte kicked out, narrowly missing his belt buckle.

"That's enough of that," she huffed. "You just proposed to my best friend."

Charlotte's heart was doing fine. She didn't appear to have any broken bones. Collin wasn't so sure of her mental faculties. What did his proposal have to do with her examination?

"I never took you for a two-timer Collin Hunsford."

Two-timer? Two what? Collin took a closer look at the situation. He was hunched over Charlotte. If someone came upon them, it might look as though they were engaged in a lover's quarrel.

"Oh," he said when realization dawned. "It's not like that. I would never make a sexual advance toward you."

Charlotte's nostrils flared. Her chin went high. Her expression tightened. It was all the cues of anger.

"I mean, you're an attractive woman. You have

excellent proportions." Collin canted his head to look at her bust, then waist, and then hips. His mother would have said she had perfect hips for breeding. Another compliment Collin learned early on that women didn't appreciate.

Charlotte snapped her fingers. "Eyes up here."

Collin snapped his gaze up to Charlotte's face. The center of her pupils were actually hazel. Much like his horse's. Though Charlotte's brown depths weren't fathomless. Hers sparkled like a match had been lit from within. The shine intrigued him. But he'd learned it wasn't nice to stare, so he averted his gaze.

"You're a very pleasant woman to look at, Charlotte. But I'm not making a pass at you. I want to make sure you don't have any broken bones or strained joints after that fall. With those very clear intentions, may I touch your body for medical purposes? Not for any pleasure at all."

Her frown deepened. But she nodded. Collin wanted to ask her which of his words had made her unhappy. He supposed it likely had nothing to do with him, and it was more to do with the fall she'd taken.

Collin took her left calf in hand. He felt along the limb for breaks. There were none. When he pressed his palm at the base of her spine, Charlotte inhaled sharply.

"Did that hurt?"

She pressed her lips together, avoiding his gaze. "No, it's fine. I'm fine. I can walk."

She didn't take his offered hand as she stood. Still, Collin kept both his hands at the ready as she wobbled to standing. Now that the human was fine, he turned his attention to the horse.

Lefroy hadn't gone too far. He and Equus had their heads together as they munched on the tall grasses. Lefroy continually shifted his weight.

"There's something going on with his leg. I'd like to take a closer look."

"Yeah, well, I can't give you that permission," said Charlotte. "I'm not his trainer."

Collin sensed something in the way she said it. He didn't know what. She was actively hiding her emotions.

Though he was almost certain he detected sadness. Which seemed right. Like him, Charlotte loved horses. So she was likely distressed over Lefroy's state. She was also favoring her right leg.

"You can't walk on that leg, and Lefroy shouldn't handle your weight. I'll take you back."

"To the Bennetts? No, you can't."

"Can't? Have I been banned?"

"No, of course not." But her expression screwed, as though she wasn't sure.

Collin wasn't sure either. He was certain Elizabeth had no interest in seeing him again. Her scrunched features and raised voice were clear indicators. Still, he didn't understand what he'd done wrong?

Then there was Mr. Bennett, who'd spoken quietly and calmly to him. But his words had been to leave. Communication was just so confusing to Collin. Even now, Charlotte, whose expressions had always been clearly written on her face, was trying to mask her emotions.

Then those dark eyes connected with his. They pierced past Collin's own layers of protection, trying to see into the heart of him.

"Aren't you embarrassed?" Charlotte asked him.

Collin didn't feel embarrassed by Eliza's rejection. No one had laughed at him. What he felt was irritated that he'd have to find a new woman to court. He doubted either of the other two Bennett sisters would accept his proposal.

He'd thought about going online to find a compatible woman. Most dating sites boasted of algorithmic matching capabilities. Though that would still require a sifting through potential candidates and then going on at least two dates. Collin was hoping to have everything in place for his rehabilitation ranch by the start of the Pemberley Races, where he could advertise his services to the racers and horse owners. That was in a week.

It was looking less and less like he would meet that deadline, which would mean another year before his business could take off. And in the meantime, he still had animals he needed to care for and low funds. Collin never turned away an animal in need. These days he was practically paying owners to care for their animals. He could never say no. Not one another creature who had trouble communicating its pain looked this way.

Right now, he had two creatures in pain. Both Charlotte and Lefroy were ignoring the signs of their injuries. Collin went into action.

CHAPTER FIVE

efore Charlotte could protest, Collin hefted her up and onto his horse. And then there was no protest in her. Equus was a beautiful stallion. His coat was midnight black, so dense it shined, just like in her favorite storybook, *The Black Stallion*.

Stallions made good race horses because they had a lot of energy. Charlotte could feel the power of the horse beneath her, just waiting for the chance to prove his speed, his prowess, his ability. She felt the exact same. Except they were both standing still.

She picked up the reins. It would only take a tug of the strap, a press of her calves, and they'd be off. Running so fast, so far that no one could catch them and bring them back to the stables, where they'd have to hold still, keep quiet until they were let out to pasture again.

It was all within her grasp. Her hands tightened on the reins. She stiffened when she felt another powerful body climb up behind her.

Collin.

Charlotte had ridden double before. But she'd never ridden a horse with a man. She'd never had a man's chest pressed against her back. Or her front. She'd never even been hugged by a guy.

Well, that was happening now.

Through his thin t-shirt, Charlotte felt the lines and ridges and indentations of each one of Collin's six-pack abs. She curved her back, which only served to press her shoulder blades into the cushion of his pectorals.

Two strong arms came around her. Brawny biceps boxing her in. She was trapped.

When Collin's calloused fingers brushed her hands, she hissed. Not out of pain. There had been a zing of energy in his touch. It shot through quick as lightning and made her sit up straight.

"Pain?" he asked.

"No." Charlotte's voice sounded strained. It had been a struggle to get out that single syllable. "I'm fine."

She was not in pain. She felt embraced. Sheltered. Secure with Collin surrounding her.

His right hand laced over the top of hers. The calluses on Collin's fingertips matched the jagged edges on her own hands. And yet, somehow, his touch was gentle. So gentle that when he urged the reins from her hands, she let him take control.

With a squeeze of his calves, Collin urged Equus into a walk. Lefroy followed their lead. His gait even now that he didn't have a rider.

Charlotte felt a twinge of guilt that she'd added to the horse's injury and discomfort. Her aunt's voice sounded in her head that she was a burden who needed to keep still and quiet.

"I can walk," said Charlotte. "I can walk Lefroy back. You don't have to—"

"Didn't we already have this argument and proved you wrong?"

Collin asked the question as a statement. His arms tightened around Charlotte. But she was certain that was because they went down a slope, and he wanted to ensure she kept her seat.

They were quiet for a moment. In the past, that had always been something Charlotte had admired about Collin. He could sit quietly, so still that it was easy to forget that he was even there. She'd tried to mimic that at home but was continually told how she failed miserably.

Behind her, Collin's back was straight. His gait easy, as though he hadn't just been embarrassingly dumped. She knew she wouldn't have been able to hold her head up so high under the circumstances. She had to admire him. Then she realized she had to stop it with the admiration. He was her best friend's ex-boyfriend.

Then she had to wonder if a man could be an ex, if the girl in favor had never considered him dating material, much less marriage material?

"For what it's worth, I think Eliza is interested in someone else," Charlotte said.

"If that's so, I wish she had said as much before our first date."

"I don't think she's admitted it to herself."

Collin took in a deep breath, which made his chest rise and press into Charlotte's back. When he sighed, that breath of air tickled the hair above her ear and sent a heated shudder across her shoulders.

"I'm… confused," said Collin.

"Heartbreak will do that to you."

"Heartbreak? I've never understood why people think the seat of emotion is in the heart. Emotions stem from the brain. I presented a logical proposition that would benefit us both. Elizabeth refused. It's my brain that's scrambled due to the illogic of the situation."

Trust Collin Hunsford to turn any romantic notion into a logical argument. It was kinda hot. The logic. Not the man.

"Women are so confusing to me," he said. "People in general, but women specifically."

"I tried to tell Eliza, love isn't logical," Charlotte said.

"Love? Is that what she wanted?"

"That's what every girl wants."

"Including you?"

Charlotte opened her mouth. Nothing came out. Because she hadn't had those thoughts about boys like Eliza and her sisters had. She'd never been the girl to write her name plus any of her male class-mates or boy band pretty boys. She'd been more interested in learning to write addresses of the homes for sale in the community in her journal. The sprawling ranches and multi-storied family dwellings that could belong to someone with a handful of cash. That's what she dreamed of lending her signature to.

"I always thought you were a logical person," Collin said.

"I am," Charlotte said. "I don't ever expect I'll fall in love."

"Neither do I. But I have to get married."

"You have to?"

He didn't answer for a long time.

Charlotte had the urge to twist in the saddle and get a look at his face. But Collin often wore a mask. Not because he hid his feelings. More so because his brain was often too busy processing the facts of a situation to consider the emotional impact.

"Well, if you're still after Eliza, you should know she does expect to fall in love. She wants passion and adventure and romance."

"Hmmm."

The sound traveled down from the crown of Charlotte's head. It skittered over her neck and spread across her shoulders.

"All I have to offer is the sanctuary of a good home, financial security, friendship, and partnership. Are you all right, Charlotte?"

Charlotte's body had listed to the right, redistributing her weight on the horse. Collin's strong arms prevented her from toppling to the ground. She'd swooned at that proposal. It was everything she'd ever dreamed of. Too bad it wasn't meant for her.

The Bennett Ranch came into view around the

next bend. The land had been in the family for generations, but the California-style ranch house had been rebuilt for the late Gardenia Bennett. The one-story home looked as though it was a part of the landscape.

The wide-open spaces outside the house were where Charlotte had learned to run. She'd learned to shout. She'd learned to ride.

The wide-open spaces inside had always been a warm and welcoming haven for Charlotte. It was the only place she'd felt like part of a family. The complete opposite to her aunt's cold apartment where Charlotte had had to sit still, be quiet, and know her place.

Charlotte needed to get back inside. She'd promised to share a tub of ice cream with Eliza over the breakup-that-wasn't. She saw Eliza coming out of the house now. Though it looked as though she was walking out against her will. Sure enough, Lydia was shoving her older sister onto the porch and down the steps. Jane brought up the rear. They nudged their sister toward Jane's car.

Eliza's steps became less stuttered the closer they got to the driveway. She wrapped one arm around Lydia. The other around Jane. The three redheads were smiling and laughing as they got into the car.

They couldn't see Charlotte or Collin at this angle and distance. They were likely headed into town for ice cream or some other such sisterly bonding. Eliza likely had forgotten that she was supposed to have that ice cream with Charlotte when she got back. That often happened when they made plans and something else came up.

"Do you want to catch them?" asked Collin. "Equus can make it to the end of the drive before they get there."

"No." Once again, Charlotte struggled to get the word out. "No need."

She didn't want to put Collin through the embarrassment of seeing Eliza again right after she'd dumped him. She didn't want to remind Eliza when she'd clearly forgotten all about him already.

Best if Charlotte caught up with her best friend when she and her family got back—whenever that would be. She could just hang out in the stables with Lefroy until they did.

CHAPTER SIX

ollin pulled up to Pemberley Ranch. The sprawling ninety-acre ranch was the largest in the whole county. It had been in the family since his English ancestors had crossed the ocean centuries ago. The large mansion looked like something out of a gothic painting, nothing like the one-story ranches that made up most of the community. Despite its size and majesty, only one person occupied the home full time. And that man strode toward Collin now.

"Collin." Fitz Darcy tipped his well-worn cowboy hat in greeting as he came toward Collin.

The two men were of equal height, both standing over six feet tall. They were of equal build, both having spent most of their lives working out of doors with animals. The same dark hair, light eyes, and patrician nose used to look down upon others had been passed on to them from some English nobility.

Collin only looked down his nose because he was taller than most everyone in town. Where he and his cousin differed was in that Collin preferred not to make eye contact, where Fitz could stare a man down until he whimpered. Holding someone's glance was stressful to Collin. When his mother and aunt forced him to do it as a child, he often got too distracted trying to hold someone's gaze that he missed the words coming out of their mouth.

Fitz never forced Collin to meet his gaze. He never forced him to do much of anything when they were kids. He was content to sit in silence, reading a book or writing letters. That silence and apathy were the primary reasons why the two of them got on so well.

"Is that you, Hunsford?"

Collin had missed the blond man walking behind Fitz. Well, not so much as missed as dismissed. Collin had nodded a greeting in compliance with the manners instilled in him. He hadn't thought more was necessary. By the use of his last name and the way the man came at him with open arms, Collin saw that he was wrong.

"It's me," said the blond engulfing Collin in a bear hug. "Carlos Bingley, you remember me?"

Collin stiffened in the hold. He stared at his cousin over Carlos's shoulder. Fitz shrugged. It was his version of an apology.

Collin did remember the man who was clapping him hard enough on the back to elicit a cough. The overly friendly friend of Fitz, who often filled the silences the two cousins had never minded. They'd met Carlos Bingley in summer camp one year. The man was a magnet for all forms of social activity. He'd latched onto Fitz, proclaiming the two of them to be best buddies. Fitz, who easily evaded any unwanted attention with a glance down that noble nose, hadn't been able to get rid of Carlos since. Collin concluded it must be because his cousin hadn't wanted to.

"I thought you had moved to Hollywood," said Collin when Carlos finally unhanded him. Collin had seen the man's face on the magazines at the checkout stand in the grocer's. The headlines were often in Spanish, which Collin couldn't read. But Carlos was always smiling that friendly smile, so he assumed the news about him was good.

"I did," Carlos said. "My show is on hiatus for the summer. So I decided to get in a little R&R for a few weeks. This is the perfect place to do it."

Collin frowned at the confusing answer. R&R had so many meanings. It's why he didn't like abbreviations or nicknames. It left too much open to interpretation, where Collin liked clarity.

Rest and relaxation? If that's what Carlos needed, he wouldn't find it at Pemberley over the next few months. It was the start of the Pemberley races, which was the biggest event of the season. And it all centered here on this land, day in and out.

Rest and recreation? If that's what Carlos needed, he definitely would find it here. More than horse racing would happen over the next few weeks. There would be a rodeo, a beauty pageant, and even a ball.

Perhaps he meant rest and recuperation? Or rest and reconnaissance. In the end, Collin realized he didn't much care why Carlos was here. Only that he wasn't manhandling his person any longer.

"We're glad to have you here, Carlos. With your celebrity, you'll be a nice draw for all the festivities."

Collin hadn't heard Aunt Catherine come up behind him. Though the woman was in her sixties, she moved as agilely as someone in their prime. Her silver-gray hair was a cloud around her head, which softened her features. Collin knew that beneath those gray and white locks was a shark.

"Oh, I'm just here as a friend, Ms. D. I'm gonna keep out of Darcy's way."

"Nonsense," she said, snaking an arm around Carlos's bicep. "Three strapping young men of marriageable age, the mamas of Austen Valley would hang me out to dry if I didn't parade you all in front of their daughters."

Collin had never seen Carlos Bingley frown. He didn't so much as frown at Aunt Catherine's words as he looked green behind the gills.

"Speaking of marriage, I thought I was going to hear wedding announcements from you, Collin."

"I thought so, too," Collin muttered.

With her attention on Collin, Carlos tried to pull away. He learned quickly that Aunt Catherine was not in any way as feeble as she appeared. She held fast to his arm.

"If you want your full inheritance released to you, you'll need to have a Mrs. to help you run Rosings. How are things going with the Bennett girl?"

"Bennet?" asked Darcy. "Which Bennett girl?"

"Have you asked her?" asked Aunt Catherine.

"I did," said Collin. "She said no."

"She said what?" Aunt Catherine dropped Carlos's arm, and he dashed away behind Fitz.

"Who said what?" asked Fitz.

"I'm not surprised," Aunt Catherine went on. "Those girls went too long without a mother's touch. Too much fire in them, especially with that red hair. Find a brown-haired girl. They're much meeker."

Collin eyed his aunt's bone straight hair. There were still a few strands of dark brown in the abundance of gray. Collin was preparing to reject that thesis when a dark-haired woman popped into his mind.

Charlotte Lee had brown hair. It might even have been black. Though she'd been raised without a mother as well.

"Same with you, Fitzwilliam," Aunt Catherine was saying.

"I'm not marrying." Fitz turned back to Collin. "Which Bennett girl did you say?"

"Not a Bennet for you," said Aunt Catherine. "I have the perfect girl for you. Her name is Ann, and you'll take her to the Pemberley Ball."

"I'm not getting married," said Fitz.

"You will if you want the balance of your trust fund. I'm still a signee."

"Keep it." Fitz shrugged. "I make enough from the Pemberley Races to more than afford my lifestyle."

Aunt Catherine pinched her lips in the expression Collin didn't need a manual to tell him was displeasure. "Are you both just waiting for me to die? I outlived all my brothers and sisters. You'll be waiting a long time."

She crooked a long, gnarled finger at both of them. The nail was sharp, much like a shark's tooth. She turned on her heel. The edge of her skirt billowed like a fin in the water as she headed into the house.

"What's this about you and the Bennetts?" asked Fitz.

"Bennett?" said Carlos. "Red-haired girl, tall with soft green eyes and a killer smile?"

"That would be Jane," said Collin. Whenever anyone talked about a smiling Bennett, they were always referring to Jane. Eliza often wore a pinched expression with a brow raised. Lydia often smirked with her gaze narrowed. Collin often had a hard time reading the sisters' expressions.

Not Charlotte's. The only way he'd known he had made missteps the other night was due to her expressive face.

"You're dating Jane Bennett?" asked Fitz.

"No," said Collin.

"So, she's not seeing anyone?" asked Carlos.

"Who?" asked Fitz.

"Jane," said Carlos.

"I don't know if Jane is seeing anyone," said Collin. "I was dating Eliza."

"You were dating Eliza Bennett?" asked Fitz. His jaw went slack as he gaped at Collin.

"I proposed to her last night."

"You're going to marry Eliza Bennett?" said Fitz. His slackened jaw tightened as he glared at Collin.

"She said no. She said a bit more than that and rather harshly."

"Now, that sounds more like the Eliza Bennett I know," said Fitz.

"So, Jane isn't dating anyone?" asked Carlos.

Collin should've set his sights on Jane. She was a pleasant girl. Much more quiet than Eliza. Possibly a little too quiet. Though Jane did smile quite a lot, her smiles weren't always clear. Not as clear as Charlotte's expressions.

"What do you think about Charlotte?" asked Collin.

"Charlotte?" said Carlos. "Is that the little sister?"

"No," said Fitz. "Charlotte Lee. She's excellent

with horses. I expect she'll be the Bennetts's new trainer now that Bert's retired."

"No, not as a trainer," said Collin. "As a wife."

It was the silence that brought Collin back around. He'd learned that silence was not often a good thing when he was in polite company. One should always be making conversation. If not him, then someone else. That someone else should've been Carlos, but the man's brows were raised. Was that surprise on his face?

"You're thinking of marrying Charlotte Lee to get Aunt Catherine to release your inheritance?" asked Fitz.

It was logical. Charlotte was mostly quiet. Excellent with animals, from what he remembered of her back in school. And, unlike Eliza, Charlotte didn't believe in the notion of love and romance.

"You know who she is?" said Fitz. "She's Eliza Bennett's best friend."

Carlos clucked his tongue. "You don't do that. You don't date your ex's best friend."

"He's right," said Fitz. "It's a rule."

"In what law book?" asked Collin.

It was a serious question. Collin already had his phone out, thumb poised to type in the Google search bar. The two men looked at each other in that way where Collin knew he'd missed something.

"You won't need to worry about Aunt Catherine if you ask Charlotte to marry you," said Fitz. "It's Eliza you'll have to worry about. She'll likely kill you."

"Eliza isn't interested in me," said Collin. "She said so herself."

"If I know anything about women, it's that they don't care until you show interest in another woman," said Fitz.

"I'm not trying to make anyone jealous," said Collin. "I'm not trying to elicit any emotion. Just a logical transaction in the form of marriage."

Again Fitz and Carlos looked at one another. Collin was done with the voluminous looks. This time he was certain he hadn't miscalculated, and soon he'd present his case to the woman herself.

CHAPTER SEVEN

The sound of squeaking brakes nudged Charlotte into alertness. But it was the creaky suspension that rocked the passenger chair forward that brought her awake. When her eyes opened, she was no longer out near the countryside. Green had given way to black asphalt. There were no vibrant red brick or aged wood structures. Instead, concrete buildings stood five or more stories tall at every corner, blocking the beautiful Montana skyline. The drabbest of gray complexes framed the car window where Mr. Bennett had pulled in.

Like always, he hadn't even set the truck in park. His boot simply pressed firmly on the brake as he smiled over at Charlotte, waiting for her to climb out. Charlotte gathered her overnight bag, fingers clutching the frayed straps. It had been Eliza's bag once upon a time, but she'd outgrown it and handed it down to Charlotte.

"Thanks for the ride, Mr. B."

"Anytime, my dear. Though I assume, we're getting close to the last of our Sunday morning rides."

"Why's that?" Charlotte asked.

"Now that you've finished your courses and are a graduate, I'm sure you'll be moving on. I'm surprised you haven't accepted an offer yet."

That's because there hadn't been any offers. Because the only job she'd ever even considered had already been given away.

"I'm very proud of you, Charlotte. Just as though you were one of my own daughters."

Just as though. But not actually. Because unlike his daughters, whom he employed, he'd made no offers to Charlotte.

Charlotte forced a smile as she reached for the handle. "Thanks again, Mr. B."

She watched as the truck pulled off and down the road. Then she turned and looked up at the apartment building she'd spent all of her life in.

Charlotte was exhausted. The Bennett girls had

come back late last night from their excursion into town without her. Eliza had passed Charlotte a tub of vanilla ice cream—her favorite. Then they'd stayed up gabbing even later into the night. They were sleeping in this Sunday morning. Since Mr. Bennett got up with the crows, Charlotte was up and back at her aunt's home.

Not her home.

She looked up at the one-bedroom apartment. There was an AC unit in each available window, even though the unit had central air. Aunt Norah always swore it was too hot, even in the winter. Charlotte's chattering teeth often woke her in the night. Either that or her aunt clanging around in the kitchen woke her in the early morning hours.

Her aunt would be up and in the kitchen now. With the open floor plan, and Charlotte's bed being the lumpy couch just a few dozen feet away from the stove, she wouldn't be able to get back to sleep. Charlotte tried to be out of the house by morning and out all day. It was harder on the weekends, especially now that she was out of school with nowhere to be.

Because she had no offers.

Now she'd have to search one out. Surely, someone in this town could use a ranch hand with only after school and volunteer experience on a ranch and one college internship. She'd happily sleep in a barn for free at this point. She couldn't spend another cold night on her aunt's couch.

"Charlotte?"

Charlotte jumped at the sound of her name. "Collin? What are you doing here? Are you looking for Eliza?"

"No," he said, stepping out of his truck. "I want you."

Charlotte raised her hand to wipe at her eyes. Then she dug her index finger into the corner to remove the crud there. Though why she was clearing her eyes when she was hearing things was beyond her. She was really tired.

"I have a proposal for you."

Now she moved her hand to her ear. She pressed at the skin of the opening of her ear a couple of times. After it popped a few times, she could be certain she was hearing properly.

"I'm sorry, what did you say?"

"I want to talk to you about a proposal."

"For Eliza?"

"For you."

"Me?"

"I'd like to offer you my hand as a partner in life."

Charlotte must be really, really tired. She was having déjà vu. Though it was someone else's déjà vu. Collin had said the same thing to Eliza the other day.

"You just proposed to my best friend less than twenty-four hours ago."

"Eliza rejected my proposal. After some reflection, I think I understand why. Eliza's a very emotional woman. You're not. I'm proposing to you a union based on economic matters, not emotion."

Charlotte wiped again at her eyes. Not because a tear had formed. Because it itched after removing the sleep crud from lack of rest.

Her palms came away wet. Not because any tears dripped down. Because of the sweat coming out of her on this cloudy day.

Her heart skipped a beat. Not because the organ was in any danger of falling. Because Charlotte was standing with her two feet planted firmly on the ground.

"Why are you doing this, Collin?"

She didn't dream for one second that Collin was actually interested in her. Maybe this was some kind of a joke like Eliza had said? A bet between him and Fitz Darcy? Though it didn't fit either man's character.

"You said yesterday you would never make a pass at me," she said.

"I'm not making a pass at you. This has nothing to do with sexual attraction. This is logical."

Which somehow didn't make it any better. Charlotte had never been one to inspire romantic feelings in any man. Now that she was sparking one's rational sensibilities...? Well, nope. Still wasn't any better either.

"I need a wife in order to come into my full inheritance so that I can turn Rosings into a full rehabilitation ranch for retired racehorses."

Charlotte had already wiped her eyes and cleared her ears. She was hearing Collin correctly, and this was truly happening. She still felt dazed as she looked into his earnest blue eyes. There was no light of desire there. No passion or interest. It was the same look he'd give to an animal he was treating, trying to determine how best to save it.

Could Collin see that Charlotte needed saving?

"I miscalculated with Eliza," he was saying. "Logically and practically, you are the best woman for the job. You don't expect love, which is something that I can't offer."

Charlotte had said that. She had meant it. She didn't expect anyone to fall in love with her. Not when her sole family member, her own flesh and blood, had never been capable of caring enough to give her an actual bed.

"Eliza lives in a big house with her family. Where I'm given to understand by the floor plans available at City Hall that you live in a one-bedroom apartment, which can't be very comfortable."

"You looked up the floor plan of the apartment building?"

"I was very thorough this time," said Collin. "I have plenty of rooms at Rosings. You could have your own bedroom, plus a sitting room for your own particular use."

"My own room?"

"Plus a sitting room for your own particular use. My mother used it to knit. Though you could use it for whatever you wanted."

"Whatever I wanted?"

"This is what I have to offer in a union, Charlotte; a home, financial security, and friendship."

It was an offer. It was her only offer. It was more than she'd thought she would ever be presented with.

"I'm sure you probably have other offers," Collin went on. "If you want to think—"

"I don't."

"You don't?" Collin pursed his lips together. "You're rejecting me, as well. I thought I'd thought through all the variables this time."

"No! No, I'm not rejecting you. I want... I want to think about it."

It was an insane thought. Marry Collin Hunsford. The man her best friend had been quasi-dating. The man her best friend had definitively dumped. The man her best friend positively did not want.

And now he wanted Charlotte. Not for love. This would be for business. Like a job.

"Would you like to come and see the rooms?" he asked. "To do your due diligence as you consider my offer?"

Charlotte looked again to the second-floor apartment. The water dripped from the AC unit hanging out of the living room window. Her room. Which wasn't really her room. Had never truly been her room. But if she went with Collin, she could have her own room and a room for her own particular use.

"Yes," she said. "I think I should do my due diligence, at the very least."

CHAPTER EIGHT

ollin pulled into the drive of his home at Rosings Ranch. The tightness in his chest relaxed as he looked up at the home of his youth. Here, in this wide-open space filled with flora and fauna, he didn't have to struggle to understand the world around him.

Flowers needed only water, soil, and sunlight. The animals needed much of the same. They didn't arrange their features into masks that Collin couldn't decipher. They didn't compose words into puzzles whose meanings were a mystery.

Rosings was a haven. Not only for Collin but also for the horses he planned to bring here. By bringing Charlotte here, he could finally put that plan into motion.

Charlotte had drifted off not long after she'd clicked her safety belt into place. Collin knew that the gentle rocking movement of a vehicle in motion was a recipe for dozing. He'd always thought that recipe was for children.

Looking over at Charlotte's reposed features, she did look child-like. Innocent and trusting in her sleep. The angles of her face were a study in symmetry. From the curved hyperbolas of her eyelashes to the right angle of her straight nose, down to the symmetrical acute angles of her mouth.

Her face had always made sense to him. Her smiles were clear cues in a world of distraction. Her words definitively denotative where he found the connotation of others confounding.

Charlotte made sense. A union between them made sense. Now he just had to prove it to her.

"Charlotte?"

She didn't budge. Only let out a little sigh and burrowed deeper into the seat. It was then that Collin noticed the dark circles under her eyes. He should probably let her sleep. But wouldn't it be best for to sleep in her own room inside the house? It was his strongest selling feature to get her to agree.

"Charlotte?" This time he put a hand on her

shoulder and gave her a nudge. "We're here. We need to get out of the car."

"But it's so warm in here."

"Wait until I get you in bed."

Her eyes flashed opened at that. Her cheeks flushed, and she jerked from him. The look on her face told him that he'd misstepped. But how?

"Oh, no-no. Not in my bed. In your bed. Remember, I said you'd have your own room. I'm not inviting you into my bed."

She winced.

Collin thought it best he stopped talking about the sleeping arrangements. This wasn't going to be that kind of marriage. He climbed out of the truck and went around to her side. Opening the door, he offered her his hand, as his mother had taught him. She hesitated again, but only for a second. Carefully, she placed her hand in his palm.

The first thing Collin felt was a shock of cold. Her fingertips were like icicles. But not for long. The chill melted as soon as he curled his fingers around hers. With the frost gone from her, a tendril of warmth spread across Collin's wrist.

The feeling was a cup of hot chocolate on a January evening. It was a toe dipped into the lake on a June afternoon. It was urging a horse into a gallop on a cool September morning.

Looking into Charlotte's eyes, Collin sensed she'd felt it too. He wondered how she would quantify the thing that had just passed between them? He wanted to ask, but she pulled her hand away, and the feeling went with it.

"So, this is Rosings," she said, stepping away from the truck.

"You've never been?"

"I was never invited."

That didn't surprise Collin. His mother had had very few guests over. Collin did most of his work on other ranches, so he had even fewer guests over. He liked the look of Charlotte standing on his land, surveying what he had built. He wanted to tell her about his plans for expansion. And so he did.

They walked away from the house as he pointed out the east pastures, where he planned to build a track to retrain the behavior of racehorses. To teach them things like a pull on the reins now means to slow down, not speed up. To the north, Collin planned to build more stables to house the new residents he hoped to buy at the Pemberley auction. And there was more fencing that needed to go up in the west as a place for horses just to roam free with nothing more to do than eat their hay.

Charlotte listened to all of his plans. She nodded. She bit at her lip. Every so often, she smiled. A small smile that didn't produce any crow's feet at her temples, but it looked genuine.

Collin liked it best when she smiled at his plans. It was clear she was interested in his project. He wondered what was behind her pensive looks and the times her perfectly angular face crinkled. And so he asked.

"You haven't thought of storage space," she said. "You've maximized for care and training, but all that equipment will have to go somewhere. If you build the barn with a gambrel, that could be one solution. You could store some equipment under the pitched roof. You could also add an extra stall or two for storage and easy access."

"I hadn't thought of that. Your idea will save me thousands, enough to buy another horse and hire on a ranch hand."

"You're going to hire a ranch hand?" she asked.

"With more horses, I'll need the help."

"I could do it."

"You?"

"Yes, me. Why not me? I have my B.S. in Equine

studies. I'm fully qualified to train horses, teach riding, and I did a few classes in equine therapy. I don't have much professional experience, but I'll work hard and—"

"All right."

"All right?"

"Yes," Collin said. "It would be your business too, so you should have a say. That's only fair as partners."

"Partners?"

"This marriage would be a full partnership, Charlotte. Out here in the pastures, I mean. Not..." Collin waved in the direction of the house.

Most of the bedrooms faced the front of the house, not the back. His bedroom faced the back because he liked waking up looking out at the ranch. The bedroom he had told Charlotte about faced the front. It was on the opposite side of the hall from his.

Collin looked back to her. Charlotte was looking at the truck. Did she want to leave? Had he bungled this all again? Maybe he should've gotten down on one knee?

"Yes," she said, but the word was quiet, almost lost in the sound of the birds and insects having a conversation of their own in the grass and trees.

Charlotte looked up to him. The perfect angles of her eyes acute as she met his gaze. Her chin lifted high in defiance of something he didn't understand.

She swallowed, and Collin watched the undulation of her neck. Suddenly, he felt very thirsty. There was sweat gathering in the center of his palm.

"Yes, you'll marry me?" His voice did not sound like his own. The words were ones he was desperate to know the answer to.

"I want to be your partner in this business. So, I will marry you."

CHAPTER NINE

The big picture window of the bedroom looked out to the front of the ranch. Instead of gray buildings, Charlotte saw the beauty of the Montana skyline stretched out before her. Instead of horns honking or feet stomping from above, she heard nothing but the serenity of nature. It was music to her ears.

And it was all hers. There was even a door. With tentative fingers, Charlotte reached for the door handle. She gave it a shove. It moved forward until the door closed with a snick.

She was all alone. All by herself. In a room she didn't have to share with anyone. In a room where the clanging of pots and pans wouldn't wake her.

She could even sleep in the middle of the day if she wanted.

It was heaven. It was hers. With only one catch.

Collin.

She had to marry Collin.

She couldn't marry Collin.

What she wanted was to work for him. He certainly needed the help. Only a man would forget to consider storage space as he expanded.

There would be so much work to do here. It would keep her occupied all day long. Then at night, she'd get to come in this room, close the door, and sleep soundlessly.

If she married Collin.

Not a real marriage, a partnership. Based on economic matters, not emotion. Not sexual attraction, just logic.

Collin had said he needed a wife to gain his full inheritance. It wasn't an unheard-of situation in this part of the country. Though it was never as romantic as the romance novels or romantic comedies made it out to be.

The guys never looked like Hollywood heartthrobs and were sometimes missing their teeth. The wardrobe was never quite as fabulous and never tailored or dirt-free. There was never a musical montage, and the only wise voice-overs were that of the town drunk shouting nonsense about the one and only time he scored a touchdown in his senior year three decades ago.

No wonder Eliza had turned Collin down. Now he'd asked Charlotte. Just another hand-me-down.

But this was the best offer Charlotte would ever get. It was a handoff her best friend didn't want. Charlotte did. So, she was taking it. She'd deal with Eliza when she—

The ringing of her phone made Charlotte jump out of her shoes. The shoes were Eliza's from a year ago. Eliza's face flashed on Charlotte's phone. Red hair vibrant, smile radiant even through the slight crack of the phone's screen.

Charlotte covered the phone with her hand as though Eliza could see where she was. It wasn't a FaceTime call. Just a normal voice call.

She shouldn't answer. She couldn't answer. But why not?

She wasn't doing anything wrong. She was simply in her new house with the man she was going to marry because he had offered Charlotte everything in the world she had ever wanted.

"Charlie? You there?"

Somehow in her quest to cover up the phone screen, one of Charlotte's fingers had pressed Accept. Charlotte stared down at the device. Her voice caught in her throat. It was as though she'd been caught stealing a cookie from the cookie jar, even though her aunt never kept sweets in the house.

"Charlie? Are you okay? Charlie?"

"What's wrong with Charlotte?" Jane's soft voice came through the phone.

"I'm not sure? She answered the phone, but she's not talking."

"She's probably still sleeping, Eliza," said Jane. "We were all up pretty late last night."

"Can you hear her breathing?" came Lydia's higher-pitched voice.

Charlotte held her breath. Which was even more ridiculous. She should say something. Or hang up. Yeah, hanging up with the best decision.

"But Charlotte's always up with the sun," said Jane. "Even when we do sleepovers. Maybe something is wrong."

"Maybe her silence is a signal that she needs a rescue," said Lydia. "We should go over there."

"No!" Charlotte covered her hand with her mouth. It was too late. The word had already crossed over the satellite network and been delivered just a few miles down the road.

"Charlie? What's going on?" said Eliza.

"I'm awake," said Charlotte.

"I think we need proof of life," said Lydia.

"Her talking to you on the phone is proof of life," said Eliza.

"Maybe the kidnapper is making her say that," said Lydia.

"You watch way too much true crime," huffed Eliza. "Charlie, we're coming over to pick you up."

"I'm… I'm not at home."

"The library?" asked Jane.

"No."

"Well, school's out, and she's not here," said Lydia. "Where else could she be?"

Charlotte wrinkled her nose at the phone and the tone coming from the other side. There were places she could be other than her aunt's, the library, school, or the Bennetts.

"I'm at work," said Charlotte.

"You got a job?" squealed Eliza. "Why didn't you tell me?"

"Because it just happened."

"Where? Who? I'm so excited for you. We need to go out and celebrate. What time do you get off? Wait? Why are you working on a Sunday?"

"Because… Because I'm moving in," said Charlotte. "It includes room and board."

And a ring. And vows. And a slight betrayal to a friend.

"Col—the rancher I'm working for made the offer this morning and needed me to start immediately," Charlotte went on. "The rancher is preparing to take on a number of horses this week, plus an expansion of the facilities and a few modernization projects."

By the time she got to the end of the last sentence, Charlotte was breathless. She was also pacing the room on happy feet. She couldn't wait to get her hands on the reins of this new project.

"Charlie, you sound like a kid at Christmas." Eliza's voice sparkled over the phone line. "I'm so happy for you. This is exactly what you always wanted."

"It is, Eliza." Charlotte breathed in, filling her lungs until they were near to burst with joy. "It is."

Charlotte let out a happy sigh of relief. She wanted to hold on to this moment, this new beginning where her future was bright in front of her, her friend was on the line supporting her, and that mattress was waiting to welcome her into a peaceful slumber later on tonight.

"I knew you could do it. That's why when my dad thought to offer you the job here at home as the trainer, I told him to forget it."

"You… what?"

"I always knew you were meant for something else."

Charlotte was finding it hard to swallow. Her heart, which had been so full only a second ago, felt entirely deflated. Her lungs were having trouble getting air in.

Eliza had cost her the job at the Bennett Ranch? Eliza had told Mr. Bennett not to even consider her, her best friend who had been loyal and working hard on the ranch for nothing, with the hope of one day being brought on. But Eliza had decided Charlotte wasn't good enough for it.

"You still haven't told us who your employer is?" said Eliza.

"It's… he's… I'll let it be a surprise. You'll find out next weekend at the Pemberley Races."

"Oh?" Eliza singsonged the word. "I see how

you're playing this. We're competition now that you're working for another ranch."

"Yup, that's it." It was a battle to get the words out. Charlotte just wanted to get off the phone and crawl into the bed.

"Well then, Charlie, may the best woman and horse win."

CHAPTER TEN

Collin brushed downward in long strokes over the horse's mane. The animal made a soft neighing sound. Collin supposed it was a sound of pleasure. The horse hadn't had much of this kind of care from his former owner.

The quarter horse was a fairly non-descript chestnut color with a white star patch on his forehead. His front toes were pigeon'd, and his heels were lower than they should've been, which was now causing him problems in the later years of his life. But here on Rosings, he would be required to do nothing more than roam, eat, and keep the other retired horses' company.

Collin planned to bring in more company in just a few days now that he was back on plan. Charlotte had said yes. He'd have a wife. Now he could have his inheritance released. Just in time for the auction that preceded the Pemberley Races.

Year after year, owners brought both prized stock and former winners to the races. Not all those horses made off with a better situation. They might become sires for the next generation of racehorses, go to sleep forever after an injection of euthanasia, or head to the slaughterhouse.

Each year, Collin had only been able to save one horse from that fate with his annual allowance, plus the money he made as a veterinarian. But with his full inheritance, he could do so much more.

He gave the horse a pat on the rear, sending him off to wander the pasture. He pulled out his cell phone, tapping the contacts until he found his aunt's entry. Collin knew the proper protocol was to call and have a conversation with his aunt. But it was too pleasant a day for that.

His two remaining choices were text or email. With a text message, Aunt Catherine was liable to reply back almost immediately. Which would then require Collin to answer promptly. It would be like having a face-to-face conversation. But through his thumbs.

No, the best course of action was email. He could

compose a thorough update of his progress, letting Aunt Catherine know that he'd fulfilled his obligations. Before he signed off, he would make the request for the release of his funds and be done with the whole matter.

He and Charlotte could go down to City Hall in the morning. They could apply for a marriage license and be married on the same day. The bank transfer should take a couple of days. He would have the check in hand by the weekend in preparation for the auction.

His plan was taking shape. Everything was back on track. The only anomaly was the sniffling he heard coming from the stalls.

Horses didn't cry. They shed tears. But only when their tear ducts were blocked. Crying was a response to an emotion, mostly sadness, anger, or pain. There were times when humans cried due to happiness. It was a concept Collin had never grasped.

A blocked tear duct he knew how to fix. He had no idea what to do with emotional tears, sad or happy. So when he found Charlotte crying while brushing the mane of one of his mares, Collin stood frozen.

Charlotte had seemed excited about coming to

work on the ranch. He'd seen her gaze widen in wonder as she took in his spread. Her nostrils had flared in desire as she made suggestions for improvements, like a storage area. Something Collin had never even considered. Maybe these were happy tears?

But no. A closer look at Charlotte's features showed asymmetry. It was akin to the miserable smile that Collin had studied. She wasn't wincing or cringing in pain. She was unhappy. Collin wracked his mind, trying to determine why.

"Is it your bedroom? Do you not like the colors?"

Charlotte's head whipped up. She brushed furiously at her eyes, trying to hide the evidence. "The room's fine. Everything's fine."

Collin knew better. But only because it was Charlotte. As always, her features were so clear to read. She forced a smile, but her eyes told the truth.

"I need you to tell me what I've done wrong," he said. "I'm not good at guessing if I don't have all the facts laid out before me."

"Oh, Collin, no. You haven't done anything wrong. You've given me everything I've ever wanted."

"If that were true, you would be happy. You look miserable."

"Hey!" Her head snapped up, and her shoulders went back.

"Your eyes are red. Your cheeks are splotchy. Your nose is running. It all points to misery. Because it's you, I doubt it's the bedspread or the drapes that have gotten you so upset."

Charlotte pursed her lips together. A single tear formed at the corner of her right eye. Collin's fingers itched to capture it so that it wouldn't make a trail down her face. Then he wondered what that trail would feel like under his fingertips. If he anticipated the tear, he could find out.

"I don't think I can marry you," Charlotte said.

Collin's fingers clenched into a ball. He snatched both his fists behind his back. "Have I done something wrong?"

"No, it's not you. It's me."

"I don't think that's accurate. There's not a single thing you've done wrong."

"Not to you, no. But to Eliza, yes."

"I fail to see what Elizabeth Bennett has to do with the two of us?"

"She's my best friend."

Collin nodded. He waited for Charlotte to go on, but that seemed the full explanation of her misery. It still did not compute. Until he remembered his conversation with Darcy and Bingley from the other day.

"Is this the girl rulebook again? Because I Googled it. There's no such thing."

"It's real. And when Eliza finds out that I'm engaged to you, that I've moved into your house, that I'm working for you—"

"With me. You're working with me. In our home, which means it's your house, too."

Charlotte's frown drooped even farther. Her lips trembled, and another tear formed in her eye, the left one this time.

Collin stepped toward her. He caught the tear before it could fall. The moisture soaked into the pad of his thumb as though his skin was dry and he was drinking her in. He wiped until every drop of the tear was gone from her face. What was left was the softest skin he'd ever felt. Likely because he'd never held a woman's face in his hands before.

Charlotte's skin was like a rose petal. She smelled sweet, too. Something inside Collin urged him to discover if the touch and the smell matched the taste.

"She's never going to speak to me again."

Charlotte's words were a warm whisper against his palm. For some reason, the sensation made him shiver. He wanted to pull her close, certain he'd find more of that warm breeze in the soft curves of her body.

"So we have to call it off."

That brought a cold bucket of ice down over his head. Collin dropped his hand from Charlotte's face. He didn't take a step away from her. His feet refused to cooperate. He forced his brain back into action.

"Elizabeth? You're worried about Elizabeth? That she won't want to be your friend if you marry me because of some unwritten rule in a book that doesn't exist?"

Charlotte nodded. Her lower lip trembled again, but her eyes remained dry. Confusion was palpable on her face. In her eyes, Collin saw the unmistakable spark of desire. He knew Charlotte loved horses and wanted to work with them. But her lips contorted in indecision, likely over the relationship with Elizabeth that she didn't want to lose.

He didn't like his odds. Girls always stuck together. Both in the animal kingdom as well as in the human world. That's why girls often went to the bathroom together so that men couldn't thin their herd and break one of them off the pack.

Collin found himself holding his breath as he regarded Charlotte. True, he didn't want to have to start over with another woman. More importantly, he didn't think he could find someone as compatible for him as Charlotte. Even without words, he understood her more than any other person in the world.

"Charlotte, you know I'm not a romantic. But I can take care of you for the rest of your life. If Elizabeth is truly your friend, she will see that I can be a good partner for you. And that I'll do all that I can to ensure your happiness. I think any friend would want that for the other."

He'd said the wrong thing. Charlotte's lip trembled again. She shut her eyes, and a flood of tears escaped to make tracks down her cheeks.

Before he could panic, she was in his arms. Charlotte flung herself against his body. Collin caught her instinctively, pulling her close and wrapping her up tight.

She continued to cry, but her sobs didn't feel distressed. They almost felt happy. Which he did not understand. But he didn't let her go.

CHAPTER ELEVEN

It wasn't the sound of squeaking brakes that nudged Charlotte into waking the next morning. It was the feeling of pulling in gently to a full stop. When she opened her eyes, she was in the passenger seat of a truck. She came to full alertness when a tanned hand quietly shifted the gears into the parked position.

Charlotte looked over to find Collin gazing down at her. He pushed his cowboy hat up with his index finger, and his blue eyes shone at her, bright as the morning sky. More than the plush leather seats which had built-in warmers, it was his gaze that warmed her through.

"We can stop off at the store and get you new pillows if you'd like," he said.

"Pillows?" Charlotte asked, turning to brush away the crud that was keeping her right eyelashes stuck together. Then she wiped at her mouth, praying she didn't come away with drool. Thankfully, her hand came back dry.

"If you didn't sleep well last night in your bed, we can get you new pillows, a new mattress—whatever you need. I want to make sure you're as comfortable in our home as possible."

Charlotte would never tire of hearing that; our home. She had a home. Her own room as well as a bonus space. Then there were all the horses and other animals and the wide-open spaces. Also, of course, her soon-to-be husband.

She brushed a hand over the yellow sundress she'd thrown on. She didn't own anything white. What sensible ranch hand or horse trainer would? This was the prettiest item in her wardrobe.

And yes, it was another hand-me-down. From Jane this time. Though Charlotte didn't have Jane's height or curves to do the dress any justice. So it hung off her like a sack.

Still, it would have to do. It was her wedding day. A day when a girl should feel beautiful and treasured. Charlotte felt presentable and valued. It was enough.

They sat parked outside of City Hall this Monday morning. In a few minutes, the doors would open. They would go in, apply for a license, and be married. And that would be that.

"I slept very well last night, thank you, Collin. I just have a habit of falling asleep in moving vehicles."

"I hope that doesn't include when you're driving?"

"No. But I don't drive much. I've never had a car of my own."

"That will have to change. You'll need a way to get yourself around when I'm away tending to others' animals. We'll need to buy you a car."

Charlotte blinked, but when she tried to open her eyes, her lashes stuck together as though there was still a bit of crud there. "You can't buy me a car."

Collin rubbed at his chin, his brow furrowed as he did so. "Is this a Women's Liberation thing? Am I being misogynistic?"

"I…? No…? You just can't buy me a car."

"I still don't understand why not."

"It's a big gift."

"Do you want one of those Italian mini car things? They're not very practical for country living. And I didn't say *I* would buy you a car. I said *we*. The marriage license we're about to sign will entitle you to half of everything I own, which is more than enough for you to buy yourself a car with our money."

Charlotte's mouth opened and closed like a fish out of water. Because she was so far out of her depths. Collin had offered his name, his home, his business, and she couldn't forget that comforting hug he'd given her the other day.

She would've stayed in his embrace for the rest of the day and into the night. But this wasn't that kind of relationship. Emotions and physical intimacy were off the table. Even though she'd already cried on his shoulder while he'd held her.

Charlotte's heart thudded at the memory. It raced at the sight of the man sitting beside her, patiently trying to give her more than she'd ever dreamed of. She tried to quiet the mutinous beating of that organ down. She knew it was too late. With each beat, her heart was slipping from its cage in her chest… and falling.

And now, the object of her misplaced affection was giving her a car.

"American-made if you don't mind," he said. "Aside from it being our patriotic duty, the fuel system of domestic cars is beyond compare of any import. Looks like they're opening."

A woman in a long skirt and cardigan was standing on the inside of the doors to City Hall. She turned a knob and gave the door a push, the universal sign for We're Open, Come On In. Collin turned from Charlotte and opened the driver's side door.

So it looked like she was doing this. She was going to marry Collin Hunsford. She'd be Mrs. Charlotte Lee Hunsford. That gave her a thrill. But the biggest thrill was that she'd get to go back to Rosings—to her home—and get to work.

She had met all the horses this morning when she'd helped Collin bring out their breakfast. She was half in love with each one and eager to get to know them better. Then they had to prepare for more horses to come at the end of the week with the auction. It was a lot to do.

Which was a good thing. All the work ahead of them meant Charlotte wouldn't have time to pay attention to her heart when it skipped a beat at the sound of Collin's voice. She would have even less energy to give any mind to think of what this would do to her friendship with Eliza.

Giving a covert glance around the mostly empty street, Charlotte reached for the door handle, but it was already being opened by Collin. He held out his hand to her. When her fingers slid into his palm, there were no more thoughts of Eliza Bennett. Not with the warmth that infused her from Collin's touch. The connection between them was growing so powerful that Charlotte felt it tingling against her thigh.

Collin pulled away from her, and the tingling was gone. He reached inside his pants pocket and pulled out a vibrating cellphone. Because, of course, it was a cellphone and not a swarm of butterflies fluttering all around them to celebrate their nuptials.

This wasn't that kind of story, and Charlotte would do best to remember that.

Collin sighed as he looked at the face of his phone.

"Problem?" asked Charlotte.

"It's the Coppins farm. They have an old brood mare. She's past her prime, but they bred her one last time because they needed the money a new foal could bring. The mare is in labor, and she's in distress. They say it's been almost an hour."

Most foals were born after fifteen minutes of heavy labor. An hour was dangerous territory for both mom and newborn. Collin looked to the doors of City Hall. Then he looked back at his phone.

"You have to help the horse, Collin."

Relief flooded his features as he looked at Charlotte. "We should be able to make it back before City Hall closes."

Charlotte smoothed her hand over her dress. She wished she'd brought a sweater to cover her shoulders. It would be cold in the library, where she planned to go and wait for Collin's return.

"Charlotte?"

Charlotte looked up to see that Collin held the passenger side door open. He had his hand outstretched to her.

"You're coming with me."

"I am?"

"Of course. You have experience with difficult births?"

"Only textbook knowledge."

"Time to put those book smarts to work."

Charlotte placed her hand in his. There was that tingling warmth that zipped through her veins. A buzzing sounded again, but this time Charlotte knew it was all in her head—the tingles, the warmth, the feelings she was developing. And in her head was where it all needed to stay.

CHAPTER TWELVE

he sun was low on the horizon when Collin pulled up to Rosings. He was still covered in horse membrane and placenta, but he felt a sense of accomplishment from bringing a new life into the world.

It was his favorite thing to see a new foal take its first steps on new terrain. The small horse had wobbled on its bony legs. Then it had stood tall to look out on its new domain.

The animal was perfect. A beautiful coat of midnight. Bright, intelligent eyes. A white starburst on its forehead, like it knew it was destined for greatness.

He would fetch a pretty penny when he came of

age. His mother, on the other hand, was literally on her last legs. As Collin was prescribing a rest and rehabilitation regiment for the mother, who still hadn't gotten up to stand, the Coppins were asking how long before they could breed her again.

"How much?"

Collin had been trying to rein in his temper when the fierce words were spoken. Both Collin and Mr. Coppins turned to Charlotte. The anger Collin was trying to hold in was blaring loud and clear on her face.

"How much for the mare?" Charlotte clarified. She turned from Coppins to Collin. "I don't want a car. I want the horse."

Collin had never seen Charlotte Lee angry before. He'd seen her concentrating with a pinched expression on her face. He'd seen her happy and smiling, mostly true smiles, but a few fake ones now and again. Right now, she was even angrier than he was over the current condition and future plight of the old mare.

Collin didn't like Charlotte's anger. It was asymmetrical and looked... wrong. He preferred her features when they were arranged in the curved lines and angles of an easy smile. Her anger was a sharp and jagged thing that he needed to do away with.

Thankfully, it wasn't directed at him. Collin was even more grateful that he could do something about it. And that's how he wound up hitching a trailer to his truck and bringing the old mare back to Rosings.

The deed had taken all afternoon. By the time they'd returned home, the City Hall was closed. There would be no ceremony today. They'd brought a life into the world and saved another. It had been a good day.

Collin looked beside him at Charlotte. She slumped down in the passenger seat, asleep again. Her eyelids were soft curves as her lashes rested on her cheeks. Her lips were a smooth polygon of peeks and valleys, but the shape was clearly a smile.

He sat for a moment and stared at her lips. For all his study of facial expressions and the different types of smiles, he'd never kissed a woman. He'd never had the inclination to. Staring at the soft slopes of Charlotte's mouth, he suddenly had the desire to know what it felt like, what it would taste like.

His curiosity would've been satisfied had they

made their appointment at City Hall today. It was a kiss that sealed the marriage ceremony. The origin of the first kiss was a blessing passed from the priest to the groom and then the groom to the bride. Thus the phrase was born, *You may now kiss the bride.*

There really wasn't any reason to kiss beyond that tradition. Kissing was not a necessary part of breeding. No other animals performed the task in the animal kingdom. They might nuzzle a nose or touch another's face, but only humans exchanged saliva.

It was nonsensical. Yet Collin was suddenly plagued with the nagging curiosity to know what Charlotte tasted like. As though she'd heard him, she opened her mouth and yawned.

The sweet scent of her hit his nose. Not an answer to his question. It was more of a tease of something to come.

"I fell asleep again?" she asked in a groggy voice.

"You did."

"Are we home?"

Collin liked the sound of that. They were at their home. "Yes, we're home. Let's get you to bed."

"What about the mare?"

"I'll take care of her. You've had a long day."

"I want to put her up. Introduce her to her new home."

"Okay," Collin agreed. "Do you want to change first?"

They both glanced down at her dress. The yellow was now a smatter of brown dirt, yellow membrane, and ruddy red.

"No point," Charlotte said. "There's no saving this dress."

"I'll buy you a new one."

"I have no business being in a dress, not if I'm going to work on a ranch. I just wanted to look pretty for my wedding day."

"You look beautiful."

A tiny gasp escaped her lips. It tasted sweeter than her yawn. Collin had the impulse to move in closer.

There was a new expression on her face. She wasn't smiling. She wasn't frowning. Her eyes were open wide. Her lips rounded in an O.

Was that wonder?

It couldn't be? She had to know how pleasing her features were. It was another reason his gaze often rested on her. That and the fact that she was so easy for him to read.

Her features contorted into something else. A giggle escaped her lips.

For the briefest of seconds, Collin froze. But only for that second. Her laughter was a tinkling sound that skated over his shoulders. It wasn't shards of ice down his back.

"What?" he asked, because he knew that she would give him a solid, comprehendible answer.

"This should be our wedding night," she said.

"That's true," he said.

"Instead, it was my first date."

"First date? As in ever?"

"No man has ever asked me out on a date."

That fact confused Collin. With someone as bright and knowledgeable as Charlotte Lee, what were the men of Austen Valley thinking? "I'm sorry it was birthing a new horse and making a mess of ourselves instead of a fancy dinner."

"Are you kidding?" she said. "I had a great time."

Charlotte's grin was so large that it knocked Collin back in his seat. Once more, that curiosity nagged at him. Urging him to lean in and find out what her smile tasted like.

Collin felt something soft in his hand. He looked down to see that his fingers were brushing up against Charlotte's. He had no memory of moving toward her, but here they were. His index finger brushed over her thumb. She was so soft, even after all the hard work they'd put in.

"I've never kissed a girl," he said.

"I haven't either," she said. "Been kissed, I mean. By a boy," she clarified. "Or a man."

"Do you think we should try? Just so that we're prepared for tomorrow. There's that part in the ceremony..."

"Right, the you may now kiss the bride part."

"That's the part."

"Did you know that humans are the only animal on the planet that kiss?"

Collin smiled, his lips parting until he felt the crow's feet forming at the corners of his mouth to indicate a true smile. "I did know that."

"Of course you did." Her cheeks flushed, indicating embarrassment. "You know everything. You're the smartest guy I know."

"I don't know everything." Case in point, he didn't know what a kiss felt like. He did know he wanted to experience it with her.

Collin leaned in. Charlotte took a breath and then came closer. He cocked his head to the left. Charlotte cocked hers to the right. He came a breath closer and...

The blare of headlights blinded them so that they bumped foreheads instead of lips. Collin shaded his gaze and turned to look out the rearview mirror. An old pickup had pulled in behind them. It took him a moment to place the owner.

Charlotte seemed to know immediately. "It's Mr. Bennett."

CHAPTER THIRTEEN

There was a node forming at the center of Charlotte's forehead. She wondered if she was turning into a unicorn. No, that was unlikely. With her luck, she was probably turning into a minotaur.

No, that was too magical. Probably a rhinoceros. Yeah, that was more like it. A big, burly rhino with a long, pointy, guilty horn protruding between her eyes after getting knocked in the head for nearly kissing her best friend's ex and getting caught by said best friend's dad.

One glance in the rearview mirror told her that the bump on her forehead wasn't as big as she'd imagined. It was barely noticeable in her reflection. What she saw clearly was Mr. Bennett frowning back at her. She jerked away from the mirror and promptly hit her shoulder against the passenger door.

That would definitely leave a bruise.

Collin was already out of the truck and rounding the back to meet Mr. Bennett. Charlotte took a few more moments in the safety of the passenger seat. She'd fallen asleep three times now in this seat. She'd fallen asleep a countless number of times in Mr. Bennett's truck.

Great, so not only had she stepped out with her best friend's ex, she was also stepping out on the Bennett family vehicle. How much lower could she sink? Probably pretty low in the bucket seats of Collin's vehicle, which was a new and more luxurious model than the Bennetts's truck.

Except Charlotte didn't feel low. She'd felt like she was soaring just a few moments ago. Collin had been about to kiss her. After he'd insisted that their relationship remain a platonic, business partnership.

But that wasn't the most surprising thing. Collin had admitted that he had never kissed any other woman. That included Eliza. Could a man really be considered an ex if a woman both unceremoniously dumped him and had never kissed him?

If Charlotte used logic, all vectors pointed to no.

Which meant she had no reason to slump down in the passenger seat of her fiancé's truck. Which further meant she had no reason to feel shame at Mr. Bennett's disapproving frown.

She was a grown woman. Not a little kid who'd gotten caught with her hand in the candy jar. That had always been Lydia.

Charlotte had never stolen anything. She'd been asked. She'd evaluated the offer and said yes. Like a grown-up.

With that knowledge, she not only straightened her shoulders, she tilted her chin up, and stepped out of the car.

"Charlotte! What on earth is going on?" said Mr. Bennett.

Charlotte's feet hit the ground, and she felt two feet tall. She wanted to climb back inside the truck. But not into the passenger seat. She looked to the backseats where the kids sat. She wouldn't get there in time. Mr. Bennett was already walking toward her.

She looked to Collin for a rescue. He was really the one who should be in trouble. But Collin was standing at the back of Mr. Bennett's truck, looking into a trailer. Charlotte had the urge to run to his side. She'd first have to get around Mr.

Bennett, who was now standing directly in front of her.

He did not look pleased. Belatedly, Charlotte wondered if she was about to get a spanking. She knew for a fact that John Bennett didn't spank any of his daughters. His disapproving frown was enough to keep his girls in line. Mr. Bennett looked at Charlotte disapprovingly now. Charlotte could only hang her head, knowing she'd crossed the line.

"What happened to you, child?"

Mr. Bennett grabbed her shoulders with both hands. Though he didn't give her a shake, Charlotte felt jolted. When she looked up, his gaze wasn't on her face. He was looking down at her clothing. At the dirt, and grime, and blood on her clothing.

"Oh, you mean my dress."

"She helped deliver a foal," said Collin, coming to stand beside her. "She was brilliant in assisting me in the delivery."

"Of course, she's brilliant," Mr. Bennett grinned. "Our girl Charlotte here is going to make some lucky horse ranching outfit very happy."

"It's me," said Collin. "I'm that lucky rancher."

Charlotte's breath caught. Her hand crept up to her heart, but it wasn't where she'd left it this morning. It had fallen so far, so fast. Those words had been the final straw before the weight of Collin Hunsford—and all that he was giving to her, all that he was doing for her—came crashing down over her. Her poor heart had never stood a chance.

"I beg your pardon?" asked Mr. Bennett.

Though Charlotte had fallen, she wasn't quite ready for anyone else to see her slip up. She turned to Mr. Bennett. The man must not have seen them about to kiss. He must not have put the two of them together to see the truth of what was between them. Or what was at least on her side of the matter.

Charlotte knew it would all have to come out sooner rather than later. But she wanted to be the one to tell Eliza. So she decided to give Mr. Bennett a modicum of the truth.

"I work here," Charlotte said. "At Rosings. Collin offered me a position, and I accepted."

Mr. Bennet's brows furrowed. Then his entire face lit up with a grin. "That is wonderful news. Eliza told me you'd accepted a position. I thought you would be going away from us. But you'll still be here, right next door. You can still pop over for Sunday suppers."

He opened his arms to hug her. Then he looked down at her mess of a dress. His arms fell to his sides, but not before opting for patting her on the shoulders.

"Well, this is very good news indeed," said Mr. Bennett. "I hope you will seriously consider my offer, Collin. Knowing that Charlotte will be looking after Lefroy would ease my worries."

"Lefroy?" said Charlotte, finally realizing that the trailer was hooked up to Mr. Bennett's truck.

"The new trainer came in today. She took one look at him and announced his racing days are over with that injury."

The injury. Lefroy's joints. Charlotte had never gotten the opportunity to talk with Mr. Bennett about it. It had all been a whirlwind of a weekend.

"You're sending Lefroy to the Pemberley auction?" she asked.

"Not if Collin here is willing to take him," said Mr. Bennet.

Collin had already saved one horse for her today. She knew he couldn't afford to do the same for another, not before they got married, and he had his full inheritance in hand. Still, she couldn't let Lefroy go to another family... or worse. Putting a horse up for auction was a gamble that could end at the slaughterhouse.

"We'll take him," said Charlotte.

Both Collin and Mr. Bennett raised their eyebrows.

"Already taking the reins here at Rosings, I see," Mr. Bennett chuckled.

Collin stared down at her. He'd told her that her expressions were always clear and readable to him. But his had never been clear to her. He was stone-faced now as he regarded her.

"We'll take him," said Collin. "Give me until the end of the week to settle up."

The two men shook on it, then went around to unload Lefroy. From somewhere deep in the recesses of her body, Charlotte's heart skipped a beat. She felt even more certain in her choice of life partner. She just hoped her choice in partner wouldn't cost her a friendship.

CHAPTER FOURTEEN

"Where is she?"

Collin knew it wasn't proper manners to make demands before greeting someone. But unlike his aunt, Fitz didn't chastise Collin when he didn't follow proper etiquette. Today, Collin was short on time. He needed to find his aunt.

"Where's who?" Fitz asked. "Eliza?"

Fitz sat on the front porch of Pemberley Ranch. He had been bent over a mountain of paperwork before looking up to give Collin his attention. There were trailers all over the property in preparation for Friday's auction and Saturday's race. Looking down at the books, Collin saw Fitz's perfect penmanship making ticks in columns.

"No, not Eliza," said Collin. "I'm looking for Aunt Catherine. She never answered my email."

"She only answers emails on Tuesdays and Fridays," said Fitz. "Something about social media detox? She's been watching Netflix documentaries again."

"Is she inside? I want to tell her the good news."

"Good news? You can't mean… Did Eliza accept your proposal?"

"What? No."

They'd seen Eliza disappearing, walking between the trailers when they'd pulled up. Charlotte had hopped out of the truck, insisting she needed to talk to her friend. Collin had come up to the house to find his aunt and get the paperwork moving for his inheritance. Once their respective conversations were done, he and Charlotte agreed to meet back at the truck and head to City Hall.

Collin was eager to have it out with his aunt and get a move on. The sooner they got to City Hall, the closer he was to experiencing his first kiss with Charlotte. They'd been too busy settling in Lefroy and the old mare last night. They'd been too dirty as well.

This morning Collin was clean-shaven. He'd taken special care with the bristles on his chin. He didn't want them to redden Charlotte's soft skin when he finally got the chance to press his mouth to hers.

"I did not accept his proposal." Eliza Bennett stormed up the steps of the house. But her march wasn't aiming for Collin. It veered towards Fitz. "Is he going around telling people that?"

Before Fitz could answer, Eliza rounded on Collin. Collin had to take a step back. The strands of her vibrant red ponytail nearly clocked him in the nose.

"Are you going around telling people that?" said Eliza.

"No," said Collin. "I'm not."

"Are you lying?" she demanded.

"I never lie," said Collin.

"It's true," agreed Fitz. "He never lies."

"I didn't ask you, Fitz Darcy."

Collin had to step back a second time as that pony tail flew in the other direction. Eliza's hair was practically a weapon. Now, Collin was backed against the railing with the two of them facing off.

"No, you didn't," said Fitz. "Why would you when you think you're right about every matter, Eliza Bennett."

"Would you two excuse me?" said Collin. "You're

blocking my path, and I'd rather not get between the two of you."

Both Fitz and Eliza looked at the small amount of space between them. If either reached out to the other, they would be locked in an embrace. As realization dawned, they both leaped away from each other. Which opened a path for Collin.

"Thank you," said Collin, taking a step but keeping as wide a berth as possible. For some reason, he still couldn't get away. Something was holding him back. Looking over his shoulder, he saw that it was Eliza holding onto his shirtsleeves.

"I don't want you to make a scene, Collin," she said.

"I'm not making a scene," he said, eyeing the hand she had on his shirt.

"About us."

"What us? There is no us."

"Exactly."

Collin took a deep breath and let it out slowly. Frustration was creeping in, as it always did when he was caught in a social situation he didn't understand. He wished Charlotte were here to interpret this conversation.

"We're neighbors," Eliza went on. "And we'll have to work together from time to time. I don't want there to be any hard feelings since I turned down your proposal."

"Oh, that," said Collin. "There are none."

Eliza let go of his shirtsleeve. Collin took a step, but he wasn't in the clear just yet.

"He's marrying someone else," Fitz said.

Collin's shirtsleeve was caught up again. "You asked someone else to marry you?" said Eliza, rounding on him.

"Yes." Collin gave a tug of his shirtsleeve, but Eliza's grip didn't budge. "You said no."

"I said no two nights ago. You already moved on?"

"I don't see the problem?" Collin looked to Fitz for help. But his cousin was watching the exchange with a mischievous smile.

"We dated for one week," said Eliza. "You should at least take two weeks to mourn the end of the relationship."

"Why?" both Fitz and Collin asked.

"It's the rule."

"I told you there was a rulebook for dating," said Fitz.

"Eliza, I don't think you enjoyed either of our dates," Collin said. "I think you were happy to be free of my attention."

"You're still supposed to wait the appropriate time."

"Are you waiting?" said Fitz.

"That's none of your business," said Eliza.

"Collin is my cousin," said Fitz. "Which makes him family. Which makes it my business."

"Excuse me," said Collin.

"What!" both Eliza and Fitz shouted.

"It's actually neither of your business," said Collin. "In fact, there is no business because Elizabeth and I are no longer involved. Right?"

"Right," said Eliza.

"I don't see any reason to have either of us have a waiting period if the relationship was so incompatible. And I agree with you. I see no reason we shouldn't part as friends."

Especially since Eliza and Charlotte were friends. He didn't want to cost Charlotte her relationships. He'd seen the two of them together, smiling. Though, if memory served, there were times when Charlotte's smile had been a little on the dampening side.

Still, Eliza made Charlotte smile. Collin liked it when Charlotte smiled. He'd do anything to keep that genuine expression on her face. So he'd endure Eliza if it made Charlotte happy.

"That's good of you," said Eliza. "Friends, it is."

She turned to Darcy. Her smile fell, but not before Collin saw a flash, a brilliant sparkle in her eyes. That sparkle burned bright and fizzled in an instant.

Collin noted the same spark in his cousin's gaze. It was as though they were challenging each other to a duel. But because they were equally matched, they decided to draw instead.

The two nodded to each other. Darcy giving a slight bow of his head. Then Eliza turned away and stormed down the steps.

"So," said Fitz. "Who's the lucky woman? Don't tell me you got her off the internet."

"No, it's Charlotte Lee."

"No, really. Tell me who?" Fitz's smirk sobered when Collin didn't offer up another name. "Did you hear nothing I said about the rules between women?"

"There is no written rule. I did a thorough online search."

"We'll see about that when Eliza Bennett learns her ex-boyfriend—"

"I was barely her boyfriend."

"—is going to marry her best friend." Fitz shook his head, letting out a little huff of laughter. "As for

Charlotte, I'd be leery of any woman whose admiration turns from love then to matrimony in a moment."

Collin wasn't sure what Fitz was implying. He didn't care for clarification. He was going to marry Charlotte, gain his inheritance, and save as many horses as he could. That was all that mattered. And so he headed into the house in search of his aunt.

CHAPTER FIFTEEN

There was a flash of red to her right. Charlotte headed in that direction, only to come face to face with a woman in a red cowboy hat. Not Eliza.

She caught sight of another hint of red to her left. Following that trail, she bumped into a little girl with a red ribbon in her hair. Not Eliza.

Was Eliza playing hide in seek with her? Charlotte was certain she'd spotted her best friend headed in this direction when she and Collin had pulled up to Pemberley. Now every sign of red she saw was like a ghost of her friend.

Maybe it was a sign? Maybe Charlotte wasn't meant to tell Eliza her news? Maybe she could marry Collin in secret, and they could spend their whole lives without telling their next-door neighbors?

It was a fool's dream. It was also entirely untenable. Because the moment the idea popped into her head, Eliza popped up in front of Charlotte as though she'd conjured the spirit of her best friend in a seance.

"I am so glad I dodged the bullet that is Collin Hunsford." Eliza looped an arm through Charlotte's and led them away from the horse trailers.

Charlotte tripped over her own feet, unable to keep pace with Eliza. It was only her friend's grip that kept Charlotte upright and not face-planted into the ground.

"You all right, Charlie?"

"I'm fine. I'm good." Charlotte tested the ground under her feet. It wasn't wobbling. Those were her knees shaking. Her friend held her firmly, allowing Charlotte to lean on her for support.

"Can you believe Collin went out and got engaged to another woman right after he proposed to me? Probably even the same night, I think."

"No, it wasn't the same night."

"What?" said Eliza.

"What?" said Charlotte.

Charlotte wanted to confess. She needed to

confess. There was a tightening in her chest that wouldn't let any words out.

She loosened her hold on Eliza's forearm, preparing to let go of her oldest friend. But Eliza gripped her hand with her fingers, tugging Charlotte even closer as though they were sharing secrets like when they were little girls.

"That cousin of his," Eliza went on. "Fitz Darcy is the most insufferable man I've ever met in my entire life."

Charlotte's chest loosened then. But only to let a series of hysterical giggles out. It wasn't the first time Eliza had used that word *insufferable.* She'd learned it in an old Victorian romance novel. It was what the heroine called the scoundrel of a hero that she wound up falling in love with and marrying halfway through the book. Eliza never caught the irony.

"Are you having a heatstroke, Charlie? Do you need to go inside?"

"No, but there is some place I need to be."

"Is this about your new job? Wait? Is it here? Don't tell me you took a job at Pemberley? You wouldn't work for the enemy."

"No," said Charlotte. "Darcy didn't offer me a job."

Eliza let out a dramatic sigh. "I don't think I could stand it if I had to deal with that man on a daily basis. Darcy or his cousin."

"Collin isn't a bad man," said Charlotte.

"No, he's not. He's not bad. He's not good. He's pretty bland. He's the kind of man that makes you despair at the entire sex. Which is why Collin and I would've never suited. But Darcy—"

"He is good." Charlotte dropped Eliza's arm. She stopped walking completely and rounded on her friend.

But Eliza wasn't done. She also wasn't on the same topic as Charlotte. "Fitz Darcy is vain and prideful and thinks too highly of himself."

"Not him. Collin."

"What about Collin?" Eliza finally turned to look directly at Charlotte. "Why are we talking about Collin?"

Charlotte took a deep breath. She was a jumble of emotions inside, no thanks to her friend who couldn't stick to a single topic that didn't involve Fitz Darcy. "So, you don't care that he's engaged to another woman? Collin, I mean?"

"Why should I? I feel sorry for her. She'll have a life of complete mediocrity and obscurity in that house with him."

"Is that so bad?"

The idea of a mediocre life, one where she could count on every day as being consistent, was a beautiful dream in Charlotte's eyes. Collin wasn't obscure. Not to Charlotte. He made perfect sense to her, and he understood her better than anyone else. And that included her best friend of over a decade.

"That's not a life for me," said Eliza. "Only the deepest love will persuade me into matrimony, which is why I'll probably end up an old maid with you."

"I'm not going to end up an old maid."

"Of course you're not." Eliza squeezed Charlotte's hands. "The right man is out there for you."

He was. In fact, Charlotte caught a glimpse of him walking toward his truck. Collin's shoulders were back. His hat dipped low on his head so that his eyes were obscure. But Charlotte knew those eyes. They'd looked down at her with kindness, with understanding.

"It's not a life for you either," Eliza was saying. "We are going to be more. We're going to have more."

"What if I don't want more?" said Charlotte.

Eliza wrapped her arms around Charlotte and squeezed. Charlotte squeezed back.

"I know you're not romantic, but you deserve more than a comfortable home, a man of good character, and connections. That's why you have me. To be here and not let you accept the short stick of life. What would you do without me, Charlie?"

Charlotte still wasn't a romantic. She knew better than to expect a man to fall madly in love with her. She was not that kind of girl.

Even now, she was sure Collin had only suggested kissing as a practice to their wedding ceremony. She didn't expect it to be a regular occurrence.

And that was fine.

It was just fine because he was offering her everything else she wanted. Which, yes, was a comfortable home, a man of good character, connections, and a good situation in life. This was her chance at happiness, and she was going to take it.

All her life, Charlotte had allowed others to dictate her course. And she'd always gotten the short end of the stick. Her aunt shoved her into a corner of her living space. Eliza offered her hand-me-downs. She'd dictated what they would do, where they would go, who they would be friends with, and who was insufferable.

Collin had been the only person to look at Charlotte, do an evaluation, and make a plan that took into account her needs and wants. Collin had offered Charlotte warmth, not just in his car and his home. He'd offered her the warmth of his arms along with half of his worldly possessions and a say in their livelihood.

Collin's proposal wasn't a short stick. It was the life Charlotte hadn't dared dream of for herself, much less ask for. Was she going to give it up because her best friend turned her nose up at it?

"Charlie, you okay? You look flustered."

"It must be the heat."

"Yeah, your hands are warm. For as long as I've known you, they've always been cold."

Eliza smiled at her as she rubbed at Charlotte's hands as though trying to cool her down. Charlotte allowed a few more rubs, but she knew the heat would not leave her hands. She was done with being cold.

"I have to go," she said, disentangling her fingers from her friend's.

"Wait, you still haven't told me about your job."

Charlotte waved over her shoulder, but she didn't turn back. She marched forward until she was at Collin's truck. He leaned against the passenger side door, watching her approach.

"You find your aunt?" she asked.

"No," he said. "I'll tell her later. You find Elizabeth?"

"Yes, but I'll tell her later, too."

Collin opened the passenger side door. He held out his hand to help her inside. When Charlotte's palm met his, another rush of warmth infused her. She gripped his hand. He squeezed her back. The heat of his touch reached her heart. And even when he let go, that feeling of security remained. Charlotte settled into the seat, and for the first time, she didn't fall asleep as they took the drive into town.

CHAPTER SIXTEEN

"But I don't wanna be here. I don't wanna get married."

"Hush, sweetie. You're not getting married. Nonnie is."

"But I don't want Nonnie to get married." The little boy crossed his small arms over his chest and pouted until his pale cheeks pinkened. "She's my Nonnie."

"What did we say about sharing?" said the young blonde-haired mom.

The couple standing next to Collin and Charlotte laughed at the child's antics. There was a cloud of gray hair atop the old woman's head, whom Collin supposed was Nonnie. The elderly man holding her hands had wrinkled-brown skin and a bald head with splotches where hair may have once grown.

Upon closer inspection, Collin noted that only Nonnie was laughing. The grandpa-to-be holding her hands tightened his gnarled fingers around Nonnie's hands, as though he'd missed the lesson on sharing, just like Nonnie's grandson.

Collin tuned the other couple and their family out. He was far more interested in the giggle that came from Charlotte. He wasn't sure he'd heard the sound before? He'd heard Charlotte laugh a few times in passing. The sound was hearty and full from the rare times he'd encountered it. He remembered that each time it would come out of her chest like a surprise.

The giggle was different. It was soft. Lyrical. Shy, even. As though it was hiding its existence.

Charlotte gazed over at the other couple as they all waited for the judge to enter the courtroom to perform the ceremony. The wedding ceremonies were to take place before the day's trial resumed. The trial happened to be a divorce. The two parties sat on opposite sides of the courtroom, sneering and scowling at the soon-to-be newlyweds.

Collin reached out and took one of Charlotte's hands. The first thing he noted was his mother's ring on her finger. The diamond sparkled under the beam of sunlight that shone through the window. But even with the warmth on her hands, there was a shock of cold there that made him grab for her whole hand.

"You're cold."

"I'm fine," she said.

Collin brought her fingers to his mouth and blew. Charlotte gasped, her lips parting and her eyes going wide. When her gaze met his, Collin saw that hazel spark in her brown depths.

Inside his chest, Collin's heart skipped a beat. In the space of that skipped beat, his attention dipped to Charlotte's lips. Once the judge got here and began the ceremony, it wouldn't be long before Collin would get to press his lips to hers.

Collin's heartbeat sped up at the thought, pounding a rapid rhythm he wasn't sure he could keep up with. The rapid changes of pace made his head dizzy. He looked down to see that his fingers had laced with Charlotte's. Their entwined hands rested against his chest, right where his heart was thudding.

"Better?" Collin asked.

Charlotte's lips moved, making the motions to mouth the word Yes. But no sound escaped. Her breath did. With them being so close, he could taste it. The air from her lips was even sweeter than he remembered.

The older couple beside them were stealing kisses, much to the grandson's dismay. Collin wondered if he might take the same liberties with his soon-to-be wife. They had never practiced that kiss as they had planned.

Unfortunately, before Collin could make the request, the door to the judge's chambers opened. He took his place before them. With an unceremonious glance around the room, he began. "Ladies, repeat after me, please. I, state your name."

Collin tuned out the whining child. He tuned out the other couple. He tuned out the judge and focused all of his attention on Charlotte and the words she formed with her lips.

"I Charlotte Ming Lee, take thee, Collin… what's your middle name?"

"I don't have one. My mother thought they were useless sentiments of a bygone age."

A throat cleared. They looked over to the judge, who glared down at them, and then glanced at his clock.

"Sorry. I Charlotte Ming Lee, take thee, Collin Hunsford, to be my wedded husband."

There was a *rat-a-tat-tat* inside Collin's chest as his steady heart began to pound out another rhythm, even speedier this time. They were just words, his brain insisted. But the sounds of the words into his ears held power. Charlotte was speaking a legally binding contract into existence, a contract that would bind the two of them together for all time.

"To have and to hold from this day forward."

With her words, Charlotte was choosing him. She was committing herself to him. Of all the people in the town, in the country, in the world, she was choosing to stand by his side for the rest of their lives. Collin hadn't realized he'd been lonely for someone until Charlotte began speaking her vows.

"For better, for worse."

Charlotte held his gaze as she spoke the vows. From the clear expression on her face, Collin could see that she meant each word. His heart skipped another beat, like it was thrilled to know that he would enjoy looking at her face and feeling the security that came with comprehending another person. Because he would never worry over misunderstanding with her.

"For richer, for poorer."

Collin was richer because of Charlotte. This

was more than gaining his inheritance. Charlotte's ideas and improvements met at the juncture of his blindsides. Together, they would forge a better path.

Collin had always declined the use of a calculator in school, preferring to do the math long hand. From time to time, he missed a step, but eventually, he'd figure it out. He'd always seen Charlotte with a calculator, working quickly and efficiently on her problems. Now, with his long hand division and her thorough calculations added together, they'd be able to save and rehabilitate even more horses at Rosings.

"In sickness and in health, to luh... to love and to cherish, until death do us part."

Charlotte tripped over the word love. Her eyes cast down when she finally forced the word out. Collin could understand why. Love was an unquantifiable thing, as were most emotions.

When it was his turn, he repeated the vows with a sure tone. Until he got to the love part. It was a necessary word in the contract, so he said it. Cherish, on the other hand, he understood. He admired Charlotte's mind and dedication. He appreciated her hard work and kindness. She was a strong and sure addition to his life. However, by the time he vowed that only death would part them, there were tears in Charlotte's eyes.

Crying women. Collin had never been good with crying women. He avoided them at all costs.

He couldn't turn his back on Charlotte. More because it squeezed something in his chest to see her so upset. Maybe she was hurt? He was still holding her hands. Was he squeezing too tight?

No, his grip was loose. Her fingers were warm. All coldness had fled.

"You may now kiss the bride," said the judge.

Charlotte blinked the tears away. Collin still saw a trace of their evidence. She tilted her head up in permission. It was a chance he wasn't willing to pass up.

He pressed his mouth to hers. Fireworks went off behind his eyes when his lips touched hers. Her lips were pillow-soft, a supple cushion to fall into after a long day's work.

Collin's heart raced again, impossibly fast this time. He was standing still, but he felt as though he'd run a marathon. Here he was at the finish line, out of breath, with all the blood rushing from his head.

He felt like he'd won first place, a blue ribbon, a gold star. He didn't care to celebrate his victory. He just wanted to kiss Charlotte again, and then again.

CHAPTER SEVENTEEN

Once again, Charlotte didn't sleep as the vehicle drove them across town and back to Rosings. She was far too dazzled by the sparkling ring on her finger. She'd done it. She'd gotten married.

She had everything she'd never dared to dream in the palm of her hand. A home where she was welcome. A room of her own, plus one for her own particular use. Not that there was anything in particular she planned to do with it. And a job working with horses in a wide-open space where she could ride, she could run, she could shout, and she would never be cold.

"Charlotte, have I done something to upset you?"

"I'm fine."

"You're crying."

Charlotte swiped at the tears that trickled down her cheeks. More replaced the ones she wiped away.

"My mother would cry when my father upset her. Sometimes she was sad. Sometimes the tears were just to get a reaction from him."

"I would never do that."

"No, I don't think you would. Your face has always been so clear for me to read. You don't hide your feelings."

He had her wrong there. She was hiding a very big feeling from him. It was the big feeling she felt for him.

Saying those vows made it crystal clear for her. Charlotte was in love with Collin Hunsford; a man she was certain would never love her back.

"I'm feeling very emotional right now," she said. "So much in my life has changed in a matter of days. It's a lot to process."

Collin nodded at that. She knew that process, he understood. Emotions, he did not. "Are you happy?"

Charlotte didn't have to think about it. Her heart rose up in her throat and answered for her whole body. "Yes. Yes, I am."

Collin reached out a hand and caught the tear

that accompanied that statement. "How will I be able to tell the difference?"

"Just ask me."

He rubbed at her cheek, catching the last few tears from her eyelids. Charlotte relaxed into the cradle of his hand.

"Charlotte?"

"Hmmm?"

"May I kiss you again?"

He wanted to kiss her again? That was a good thing because Charlotte wanted to kiss Collin every moment for the rest of her life. If their lives could consist of horses and kisses, she would only ever cry happy tears.

"You don't have to ask," Charlotte said. "You've given me a home, a place to belong, a job that I love. You can have all the kisses you want."

Collin pulled her to him. There was an urgency in his grip that made Charlotte gasp. Could that urgency be desire?

Charlotte pretended it was as she gave herself to Collin. She kissed him with everything in herself, trying to let him know what she felt without the words. Hoping that maybe one day he'd feel something, too.

She had no idea how long they stayed locked

together. It could've been a moment. It could've been forever. It was only the knock that sounded at the car window that made them jerk apart.

Fitz Darcy peered into the driver's side window. His brow was raised high as he regarded the two of them. "Sorry to interrupt, but I brought over your wife's wedding present."

"Wedding present?" asked Charlotte.

"It's a car," said Collin.

"You bought me a car?"

"I didn't buy it," said Collin. "It's an old family car no one was using."

Charlotte had had her fair share of hand-me-downs. Nothing so big as a car. When she got out of the vehicle, Fitz placed the keys in her hand.

"It's parked around front," said Fitz. "Unfortunately, Aunt Catherine arrived as I was headed over. And she demanded to come along. She's inside."

"She's inside my house?" asked Collin.

Darcy shrugged as though to say what did you want me to do.

Charlotte had seen Catherine de Bourgh in passing. Though the two had never been introduced. Like her nephews, Aunt Catherine rarely smiled. In fact, Charlotte distinctly remembered many a person hurrying to get out of her way as she walked into a room.

"Why are you young people lingering out there?" came a smoke filled voice. "Come in here."

Aunt Catherine was in Charlotte's sitting room. Unsmiling as ever as she looked Charlotte up and down. Had Aunt Catherine turned on the AC? It was colder than when they'd left this morning. Charlotte wished she could hurry on past, up the stairs, and into her bedroom, which was warm.

Standing to the wall opposite, as far away from Aunt Catherine as he could get was Carlos Bingley. His bright celebrity smile looked a bit war-weary and wobbly. When he turned to his friends, that smile shot accusatory daggers. It was clear Carlos hadn't appreciated being left alone with Aunt Catherine.

Collin ignored Carlos. Fitz offered his friend a one-shouldered shrug.

"Is this her?"

"Aunt Catherine, this is my wife, Charlotte."

"Good afternoon, Mrs. de Bourgh." Charlotte pasted on her most winning smile. This woman was her family now.

Aunt Catherine sniffed as she glanced at Charlotte. "Not as pretty as the Bennett girl."

A blast of cold snaked around Charlotte's shoulders. She sat down on the couch across from Aunt Catherine. The other day, Charlotte had found the cushions lush and welcoming. Now they felt lumpy. A spring poked her in her thigh.

"Who are your people, girl?"

"Cheryl Lucas was my mother. My father's name was Cai Lee. They both passed away. I've lived with my aunt, Norah Lucas, since I was a baby."

"I knew the Lucases. Your aunt let you get married in that?"

Charlotte looked down at her slacks and shirt. It wasn't white. But she and Collin had planned to come back to the ranch and tend to the horses. The old mare who'd just delivered needed looking in on. And they wanted to start Lefroy on a regimen to heal the issue with his joints. That was Charlotte's purpose for the day, other than saying vows to Collin.

"We have work to do, Aunt Catherine," said Collin.

He came over and stood next to Charlotte. He didn't reach out for her. Though Charlotte wished he had. She knew his touch would've staved off the cold nipping at her fingertips.

"You're right about that," said Aunt Catherine.

"There's a lot of work to do. Namely, the begetting of an heir."

Collin stiffened, crossing his arms over his chest and keeping all his warmth to himself. "Charlotte and I didn't negotiate intimacy in our marriage. She's more a business partner."

Over in the corner, both Fitz and Carlos winced. Charlotte felt their cringes down in the pit of her stomach. Right where her heart had dropped. Now the rest of the town would know that she was in a loveless marriage. Just as she had spent her entire life in a loveless home with a family member who looked at her as a burden.

"Hmmm," Aunt Catherine sniffed disapprovingly. "Well, you've met the terms of the agreement. Your full inheritance will be released to you."

Collin nodded. A sigh of relief escaped his lips. He'd gotten exactly what he wanted.

So had she. So why wouldn't this pain in her chest stop?

Charlotte knew that Collin could never love her. He'd stated it plainly as part of their original agreement. She was the one that had changed her mind. She was the one that had changed her heart.

She didn't hear the rest of the conversation

between Collin and his aunt. She excused herself, mumbling something about wanting to change.

Inside her bedroom, it was warm, but Charlotte was still cold inside. Because just like always, she was that same orphan looking out at the world, hoping that someone, somewhere, would love her back.

She squeezed her fist, trying to rub warmth into her cold fingers. There was a grinding sound between her fingers. The set of car keys rubbed against the ring on her fourth finger.

Charlotte took the ring off her finger. She kept the keys in her hand as she walked down the steps to the front of the house and out the door.

CHAPTER EIGHTEEN

"Well done, Collin. The Lee girl looks like she'll be biddable enough."

Collin was only barely listening to his aunt as they walked her to her car at the back of the house. His mind was still on Charlotte and that kiss they'd shared in his truck. He'd rather be trailing behind her up the stairs, letting his hand rest on her low back, sipping at her lips one more time. And then figuring out how he could do it again.

"You do need stop this nonsense about no children," Aunt Catherine was saying. "This modern idea of being child-free is not sustainable. I won't see this family's wealth be left to a horse. Do you hear me?"

Collin did hear her, loud and clear. He wondered

how he could bring up the idea of children with Charlotte. He wouldn't press her. He'd be patient and wait as long as she'd like, but he'd like to leave the door open to children.

The thought of a little girl with her dark hair and that golden sparkle at the center of her eyes. Or a little boy with a smile just like his mother's. Yes, Collin liked that idea a great deal.

Just the thought of his wife round with his child in her belly made Collin trip over his own feet. The quicker he got his aunt, Fitz, and Carlos off his property, the quicker he could determine how to start those negotiations.

"I'll start the transfer process in the morning. You'll have your full inheritance at your disposal by week's end."

Fitz helped their aunt into her car. Aunt Catherine drove away in a plume of smoke. Collin walked with the other two men over to Fitz's truck. Instead of climbing in and driving off, Fitz reached out a hand to Collin.

"I never thought I'd see the day when you stood up to her. Good on you, cousin."

"I call foul play." Carlos clapped Collin on the back. It felt like a friendly gesture, not one meant to cause pain. "We didn't get to throw you a bachelor party. We're going out tonight."

"It's his wedding night," said Fitz. "Though maybe he can go, if you and your wife don't have that kind of relationship?"

"Are you kidding me?" said Carlos. "With a looker like Charlotte, that will change quick."

"A looker?" asked Collin.

"I'm not sure you've noticed, but your wife is beautiful," said Carlos. "Not to mention, we saw that kiss when we pulled up."

Back to that kiss. Just the thought of it had Collin turning back to the house. They were standing at the back, so he couldn't see the front where Charlotte's bedroom window was visible.

"Yeah, I don't think we're having a bachelor party tonight," said Carlos. "Let's get out of here, Darcy."

Before they could climb into Fitz's truck, another plume of smoke announced a new arrival. In the light of day, Collin recognized the Bennett truck. Only it wasn't Mr. Bennett driving. Two red heads climbed out when the truck came to a stop.

This was the most visitors Rosings Ranch had had all year. Unfortunately, all the traffic happened on a day when he only wanted to entertain one person. He didn't have a lot of patience left to offer the manners his mother and aunt had worked so hard to instill in him.

"My dad said Charlotte's working here," Elizabeth Bennett said as she stormed up to Collin. Her stance reminded him of an avenging angel he'd seen in a comic book. Even the wind conspired as it blew her red strands around her head, like a tornado.

"Charlotte does more than work here," said Fitz, stepping down from his truck to stand beside Collin.

"Did anyone ask you, Fitz Darcy," said Eliza. "Keep your big nose out of it."

"You think he has a big nose?" said Jane.

"Hello, Jane," said Carlos.

Jane's smile turned from amusement at her sister to the brightest Duchenne Smile Collin had ever witnessed. "Hi, Mr. Bingley."

"You can call me Carlos."

"Where's Charlotte?" said Eliza. "In the stables?"

"No, she went to her room," said Fitz.

"You know, I was wondering if the old creamery was still in business?" said Carlos.

"They remodeled it a couple years after you left," said Jane. "My friends and I go all the time."

"Her room?" said Eliza. "Right, she did say the job came with room and board."

"The job?" said Fitz.

"I still have a bit of a sweet tooth," said Carlos.

"You can come with us sometime, if you'd like," said Jane.

"Yeah," said Carlos. "That'd be great. I'd love to be your friend."

"Great." Jane's smile wobbled as though a rain cloud dampened it.

"Yeah." Carlos's smile looked a little wet behind the gills as well. "Great."

"Well, I suppose marriage is a job," said Fitz.

"What are you talking about, Darcy?" said Eliza.

"You don't know, Bennet?" said Fitz.

"Don't know what?" Eliza turned to Collin.

Collin felt a little dizzy trying to follow the two separate conversations going on at the same time. Especially when his mind was preoccupied with trying to politely ask his visitors to leave so that he could get back to his wife and renegotiate their future.

"I thought she told you the other day," said Collin. "When she came to find you at Pemberley."

"She told me..." Eliza looked between Collin and Fitz. Her gaze settled on Collin's ring finger. "You're married?"

Before Collin could answer, Eliza's gaze whipped back to the house, then back at him.

"She's not…" said Eliza, holding up an accusatory finger. "You didn't…"

Both Collin and Fitz leaned back and out of the way of that finger. Collin had never been prone to imagination. But with the fire in her hair and the sharp edges of her gaze, he wasn't so certain that Elizabeth Bennett couldn't make sparks shoot from her person.

"Where is she?" Eliza demanded.

There was a part of Collin that wanted to protect his wife. Charlotte had just had to put up with his aunt. She shouldn't have to put up with an irate Elizabeth Bennett.

"Second floor, likely second bedroom on the right," said Fitz.

With a final glare at Fitz, Eliza stormed off inside the house. Jane trailed off behind her, giving Carlos a friendly wave.

Collin turned to his cousin.

Fitz held up his hands. "Sorry, it's every man for himself when it comes to that woman."

"Most beautiful girl I've ever met, and I asked her to be my friend," said Carlos. "That's just… great."

"I think I should go and check on my wife," said Collin.

Before Collin could get to the door, Eliza came storming back out with Jane on her heels. Collin looked past the Bennett sisters for signs of the dark-haired beauty he'd married and wanted to kiss again. But there was only fire red.

"She's not there," said Eliza.

"What do you mean, she's not there?" said Collin.

Collin walked past them. He took the stairs two at a time. But Elizabeth was right. Charlotte was not in her bedroom. Neither was she in her sitting room.

Something urged him to double-check in her bedroom. That's when he saw it. His mother's ring sat on the nightstand table.

Collin picked it up and held it in his hand. It was still warm from her fingers. Coming down the stairs, he looked out the window and saw that her wedding present was not at the front of the house.

CHAPTER NINETEEN

Charlotte wrapped the blanket around herself. The high thread count didn't matter. The heavy gray blanket felt like it was made of cold.

She shifted her weight, bringing her feet up under her. A spring poked her in her heel. Another poked her in the hip. Both prevented her from getting comfortable.

Then again, she'd never felt comfortable in her aunt's apartment. It felt even more unwelcoming after sleeping in her own bedroom with a soft, full mattress and a comforter that had enveloped her in actual warmth. But Charlotte couldn't stay one more second at Rosings. Not with her new heart condition. It would be bad for her health.

Here at her aunt's, Charlotte had no illusions of being loved. She had no delusion that there would be any warmth within these four walls. The cold was almost welcome over her skin.

Aunt Norah had taken one look at Charlotte when she'd walked in the door. Her thin face had soured. Then she'd gone and shut herself in her room.

Charlotte could face the indifference of her aunt every day. Or rather, face her closed door. She couldn't do the same with Collin. Having her heart race every time he came into a room would've been the end of her.

Her heart felt barely operable now. The beats were sluggish and slow. So the banging that reached her ears confused Charlotte.

When she heard the knocking coming from across the room, she comprehended it was the door and not her chest. Her heartbeat kicked up when she realized that there was someone on the other side of the door making the noise. Could it be Collin? Had he come for her?

Her traitorous heart sped up then. It didn't care if she'd spend her days facing unrequited love. If Collin was on the other side of that door, and he reached one of his warm hands towards her, and he asked her to come back, Charlotte wouldn't hesitate.

When she opened the door, it wasn't her husband standing on the threshold.

"We need to talk." Eliza shoved her way into the apartment, then immediately shuddered. "Let's talk outside."

"No, Eliza. I'm not in the mood to go out. I just want to stay home right now."

"From what I hear, this isn't your home any longer, Mrs. Hunsford."

Charlotte averted her gaze from her best friend. She went back to the couch, sat, and pulled the cold blanket around her. More springs popped up like they were old friends come to welcome her back.

Eliza sat in the opposite corner of the couch. Then immediately popped back up. She glared down at the furniture as though she was ready to fight one of the wayward springs. "Charlie, help me understand what's going on."

"I don't want to talk about it right now."

"Too bad because I'm pulling best friend rank. That means you talk."

Charlotte let out a sad laugh. "Best friend. You know what I never understood? Why? Why did you choose me?"

"Choose you?"

"To be your friend, your best friend. Was it because I was the poor little orphan, and that made you look better?"

Eliza blinked a few times as though the cold of the room had become a living, breathing thing that fogged the space between them. "You think I chose you? I thought we chose each other?"

"You even had two built-in friends."

"I love my sisters, but they don't get me like you do. They have to love me. You choose to. Or at least I thought you did."

Eliza's hand came to Charlotte's face, capturing the tear that fell. But there were too many tears. Eliza's hand left Charlotte's face, and her arms came around her back, pulling her close.

"Talk to me, Charlie. We always tell each other everything."

"No, we don't." Charlotte sniffled into Eliza's shirt, likely leaving behind more fluids than just her tears. "You tell me everything, and I listen."

"I'm listening right now."

"Why did you tell your dad not to hire me? You didn't think I was good enough?"

Eliza pulled away. Charlotte had trouble meeting

her gaze. She tried to turn away, but Eliza gripped her forearms.

"It never occurred to me that you would settle for working on our ranch," said Eliza.

"It's all I ever wanted, to be a part of your family."

"But Charlie…? You've always been a part of our family. Since I apparently chose you to be my friend against your will."

Charlotte shook her head no. "You always dropped me back here on Sunday night."

"Well… yeah. Because this is where you lived."

"But I wanted to stay at your house forever."

"Oh, Charlie." And she was back in her best friend's arms. "I may not have listened before, but I still know you better than anyone else. And I think you want a different forever home now."

Charlotte whimpered, definitely snotting up her friend's shirt. "I'm sorry I didn't tell you. I knew you wouldn't approve."

"Of my bestie stealing my ex."

Charlotte jerked away. "He wasn't even your ex. You went on three dates."

Eliza smirked but then turned serious as she wiped away the last of Charlotte's tears. "I don't care about him. I care about you. And as your friend, I think I have a say in who is approved to date you, much less marry you. I can't believe you got married without me."

"I knew you'd talk me out of it. Or say he wasn't good enough for me. But Eliza, I couldn't do better."

"You're in love with him, aren't you, Charlie?"

Charlotte couldn't form words. She bobbed her head.

"Since when, exactly? Before or after, I dumped him."

"After." Charlotte's head snapped back in indignation.

"Good, good." Eliza held up her hands. "Just checking."

"He's my choice, Eliza."

"Then why aren't you at Rosings?"

"Because I love him, and he doesn't love me back. It's all business for him."

"I'm not so sure about that. He looked pretty panicked when I told him you weren't in your room."

"Probably because he thinks he'll lose his inheritance and the horses he plans to buy at auction. I don't want that. I want him to be able to buy the horses. I want to work there with him. I just can't live there as his wife. It hurts too much."

"Okay." Eliza stood, giving Charlotte a tug. "Let's get you packed."

"Didn't you just hear me? I can't live with my husband who doesn't love me back."

"Yes, I heard you. That's why we're going home."

CHAPTER TWENTY

Collin turned the ring over in his hand. The sparkle of the diamond in the setting sunlight didn't bring him the joy it did whenever his mother wore it. The ring shouldn't be in his hand. It should be on Charlotte's.

He should be out in the fields with her, watching her as she helped with the horses. Talking with her about the improvements they'd agreed to make to the ranch. Gazing at her as she spoke to him while he easily and clearly understood her every word and meaning because she hid nothing.

Except Charlotte was hiding now. She had gone away from him, driven off in the car that he had gifted her so that she could get around. Collin didn't understand what he'd done wrong. More than anything, he was regretting that getaway gift.

"She probably left because you didn't take up for her when your aunt was putting her down," said Carlos as he scratched Lefroy behind the ears.

"Putting her down?" asked Collin.

"When your Aunt Catherine said Charlotte wasn't as pretty as Eliza," Fitz said.

"Charlotte's not as pretty as Elizabeth."

Both Fitz and Carlos winced, letting out pained groans. Lefroy whined and shook his mane of hair. Large eyes glaring at Collin as though the horse wanted to kick him.

"Charlotte's features are entirely symmetrical. Her face is a study of angles and curves. She's wonderfully understandable, an elegant solution. Whereas Elizabeth is jagged lines of confusion."

Fitz's lips pinched into an uneven line of displeasure.

"That's good," said Carlos. "You should've said that."

"Why do I need to state a fact?" asked Collin

"Does Charlotte know that you think she's... symmetrical?" said Fitz.

Collin thought about it. He'd never said the

words out loud to her. Would he have to say all of his thoughts about her out loud?

"You also called your wife your business partner," said Carlos.

"She is my business partner. We're equal in all things."

"That's very rah-rah feminism. But it didn't sound romantic." Carlos gave Lefroy a pat on the rump, and the horse bent his head to munch on his dinner.

When had this become about romance? Collin and Charlotte had set forth very clear boundaries in their agreement to marry. They had been very thorough, and neither of them required the other to be overly emotional.

"When you find her, you need to go and make a romantic gesture," said Carlos.

"I don't see why?" said Fitz. "They negotiated a contract. She's technically in breach."

"And your aunt wonders why you're not married either," said Carlos.

"I have no interest in marriage," said Fitz.

Collin was interested in marriage. He was most interested in his marriage and making certain it worked. Somehow he'd made his wife unhappy, and that would not do. Charlotte was at her loveliest when her lips lifted in that perfectly curved smile.

"Charlotte said she wasn't interested in romance," said Collin.

"She lied," said Carlos.

"She's an honest person."

"She's a woman. All women want romance, passion, adventure."

Both Collin and Fitz scratched at the stubble forming on their chins. Lefroy raised his head and let out another whine, his large eyes fixed on the cousins. When neither man's features straightened in understanding, he gave his mane of hair another shake and went back to his hay.

"How do the two of you move through the world?" Carlos sighed. "Okay, we can go Romeo style or Lloyd Dobler."

"Romeo?" asked Collin, "As in Shakespeare? Doesn't he die at the end of that play?"

"Who's Lloyd Dobler?" asked Fitz.

"I clearly see why both your mothers put clauses on your inheritances about wives."

"I don't even know where my wife is," said Collin.

"I do," said Carlos, holding up his cell phone. "Jane texted me. Because we're friends. But I'll work on that problem after I solve yours. Charlotte is staying with the Bennetts."

"She's spending time with her best friend," said Collin. "That's a normal thing that girls do, right?"

Fitz shrugged.

Lefroy whined.

"They're having ice cream," said Carlos. "You know what that means?"

Collin shrugged.

Fitz shrugged.

Lefroy spat out a lump of quid.

"Eating ice cream is what girls do when they're going through a breakup," explained Carlos.

"Charlotte and I didn't break up. We just got married."

"We need to head over there asap," said Carlos. "What's her favorite song?"

"I don't know?" said Collin. "I'm not even sure if she likes music?"

"You married this girl without knowing anything about her?" said Carlos.

"I know plenty about her," said Collin. "I know she has a BS in Equine Therapy."

"College records are public information. Anyone could've googled that," said Carlos.

"She lost both her parents. She lived in a one-bedroom with her aunt for the last two decades. The heating and air vents are ancient in that old building."

"Explains why she was eager to marry you," said Fitz.

"Her expressions, they've always been so clear to me. Other people hide their emotions. But Charlotte's face was always easy for me to read. Whenever I was confused, and she was near, I'd look to her for social cues. It was always clear to see when she was happy, truly happy. Not a dampening smile or a qualified smile. A true Duchenne smile with crow's feet and all."

Carlos and Fitz looked at each other. Lefroy lifted his head. Instead of a whine, he let out a long neigh that sounded relaxed and happy.

"You know, I think that was verging on romantic," said Fitz.

"For you Darcy boys, yeah," said Carlos. "It's the best we're going to get."

CHAPTER TWENTY-ONE

"Tonight, we are done with boys, ladies," Eliza proclaimed, holding her spoon in the air like a sword.

"Speak for yourself," said Lydia, digging into a tub of Strawberry Tart Ben and Jerry's. "The rodeo will be here soon, and you know how bull riders react to all things red."

"That's the bull, Lydia. Not the rider," teased Eliza, digging into her Cherry Garcia pint.

"Remember what Mama used to say?" Jane scraped the bottom of her Berry Sweet pint. "Just because trouble comes visiting doesn't mean you need to offer it a place to sit down."

"Oh, like you weren't trying to climb up and have

a seat on Carlos Bingley's lap this afternoon," said Eliza.

"I was being neighborly," said Jane.

"Is that what the adults are calling it," said Lydia.

"At least I made my interest plain, instead of throwing rocks like you always do with Fitz Darcy." Jane flung a dollop of cream at Eliza's nose.

Eliza scooped up the dollop of Berry Sweet ice cream and licked it off her fingers. "I would throw a rock at Fitz Darcy, but then I'd have to actually think about him."

"Which, of course, you never do," teased Lydia.

"Shut it, the both of you. We're here for Charlie. And like I said, all men are pigs tonight."

"Collin's not a pig," said Charlotte, as she scraped the sides of her plain vanilla ice cream.

Eliza had tried to get Charlotte to opt for the Vanilla Caramel Fudge. But Charlotte had never had a sweet tooth. Even this much sugar in the plain vanilla was upsetting her stomach. Or maybe it was the ache to be back in Collin's arms.

"I've always liked Collin Hunsford," said Jane. "He has such fine manners."

"He's okay," said Lydia. "He's tall. I like that in a man."

The two Bennett sisters looked at Eliza. Her

tub of ice cream was empty, so there was no reason sweet words couldn't come out of her mouth.

Eliza took in a labored breath. "Well… Collin was always quiet. He never interrupted me when I spoke, unlike some—"

Both Jane and Lydia glared. Eliza stuck the empty spoon back in her mouth.

"Collin actually has a lot to say," said Charlotte. "If you get him talking about animals, or his ranch, or how he wants to turn it into a rehabilitation haven for retired racehorses."

"Yeah, he did talk about that," said Eliza, sticking her spoon into Charlotte's pint. "But I wasn't listening."

"He really seems to care about you, Charlotte," said Jane. "He looked panicked when we told him you weren't in your room."

But he hadn't come to find her. He hadn't called her cell phone. Jane had texted Carlos Bingley that Charlotte was with them. It had been hours, and Collin hadn't even stopped by to see that she was okay.

Charlotte didn't think it was because Collin had gotten what he'd wanted from her, and now he was done with her. Though she did believe that was a part of it. Mostly, Charlotte doubted Collin even thought to come after her.

"You were right." Charlotte turned to her best friend.

"Of course, I was," Eliza said around a mouthful of vanilla ice cream. "About what?"

"I do want passion. I'm not so sure about adventure. But I would like a bit of romance from time to time."

The spoon dropped from Eliza's mouth. "You deserve it all, Charlie."

"Collin can't give that to me."

"Can't or won't?" asked Jane.

"I don't know?"

"What are you going to do now?" asked Lydia.

"She's going to stay with us," said Eliza.

"For a while," Charlotte agreed. "But then I have to look for a job. I have to get on my own two feet."

"You can do that from my room," said Eliza.

Charlotte shook her head. She'd had a taste of independence after the night she'd spent at Rosings. She wanted to stand on her own and have a bedroom all to herself. If she wasn't going to share one with her husband, that is.

She didn't want to be the poor, unloved orphan anymore. Because she wasn't. She had never been.

Charlotte was loved, loved fiercely by the women in this room. She knew they would never let her fall. They'd be too busy urging her to eat her feelings with ice cream, and then she'd never fit through the door.

It wasn't the worst plan.

She would need to face Collin again. At the very least, she needed to return the car he'd given to her as a wedding present. She would also need to tell him to his face why she had to back out of their deal.

And then, as if she'd summoned him with a thought, Collin's face was in the window. He held a boombox over his head. Out of the speakers came the sounds of horses neighing and whinnying.

CHAPTER TWENTY-TWO

ollin almost dropped the boombox when he saw Charlotte through the window. She was smiling. It was a genuine smile as she lifted ice cream to her mouth. A mouth he'd kissed a few hours ago. He'd never been a fan of sweets, but he ached to taste the cream that rested at the corner of her lips.

Still, it was her smile he was most enthralled with. If she wasn't sad any longer, then perhaps she would come home with him? But then her smile faltered.

"Turn up the volume," urged Carlos.

"If he turns up the volume, there will be a stampede," said Fitz. "Really, horse sounds?"

"She loves horses," said Collin. "This is the

mating sounds of horses. It seems the most appropriate romantic gesture."

Fitz sighed. Carlos grinned encouragingly. Collin held the box higher, and then he caught Charlotte looking at him.

Her face was an open surprise. Like a present at Christmas the few times he got exactly what he'd wanted; a Casio graphing calculator, a vintage farriers tool kit.

Charlotte rose slowly from her seat on the pink bedspread. Collin was squinting at the brightness and pink glaring back at him through the bedroom window. But all he could see was Charlotte, her dark hair, that twinkle in her eyes, and her bright smile.

Unfortunately, Elizabeth beat her to the window. "What are you doing? Did Darcy put you up to this?"

"Not my idea, Bennett," said Fitz, chucking his thumb at Carlos.

"Oh, how romantic," sighed Jane, coming to stand to one side of the window.

"What is that sound?" asked Lydia.

"A stallion's mating call," said Collin.

Jane's sigh skittered to a halt. Elizabeth's nose wrinkled in distaste. Lydia licked her lips as she gazed at Carlos.

Charlotte's grin wobbled. She wasn't looking at Collin. She was looking down. There was disappointment in her smile.

"Charlotte, may I speak with you?"

She raised her head. Their gazes connected. Everything felt right in Collin's world, looking into the center of Charlotte's eyes and finding that spark. He would get her to explain the problem he was unaware of. He would fix it. Then they would go home.

With some pushing and shoving of Elizabeth by her sisters, the Bennetts cleared the room. Carlos and Fitz sunk into the shadows of the yard, making themselves scarce. Then Collin was alone with his wife.

He wanted to reach for her hands. He wanted to pull her into his arms. He wanted to press his lips against hers again. But the screen of the bedroom window separated them. Besides that, he was uncertain if that's what Charlotte wanted any longer.

"I didn't think you'd come," she said.

"I don't understand what made you leave? Was it that I didn't tell you that you're symmetrical and equal in all things?"

"I'm... what?" asked Charlotte. The smile was completely gone from her face now. She was frowning in confusion. That would not do. They both couldn't be confused.

"I'm messing your angles up."

"My angles?"

"Your face." Collin reached out to the window. He found the latch of the screen and pulled it down. Then he was touching her face. "It's always been so easy for me to read your face. When I'm confused, I look to you for clarity."

A tear streamed down Charlotte's face. Collin was botching it again. He was making it worse.

"Charlotte, all I know is that you're sad, and I don't understand what I did to make you sad. I don't know what I'm doing that keeps making you sad when I just want to make you happy. Tell me what to do to make you happy."

Charlotte shook her head. She was smiling as she did so. Only the smile didn't reach her eyes. The signals were mixed, and Collin couldn't decipher them.

"It's nothing you did or are doing that's making me sad," she said. "You gave me everything I thought I ever wanted. It's just that I realize I want more."

"Name it, and we'll get it for you."

Charlotte pressed her lips together as though she

didn't want any words to escape. However, one single word did. "Love."

Charlotte grinned bigger, but the pain also grew in her eyes. Collin's frustration grew. There were too many mixed signals from a face that had always read so clearly for him. Now her words weren't making sense, either.

"I broke our deal, Collin. We said a home, friendship, and a partnership. But I went and fell in love with you. I thought I could love you quietly. But I can't. When you look at me, you're going to see it in my face."

Was he? Did he? He didn't know the facial expression for love. If he saw it reflected back to him on Charlotte's face, he didn't think he'd mind so much.

"I want you to love me back."

Collin's hand fell from her face. Charlotte reached for him then, cupping his face with her soft hands. Her touch soothed him.

Was this it? Was this love? A soft caress when he was confused.

"You can't, can you?" she said. "You can't love me back."

Charlotte pulled her hands away from his face. Without her touch, Collin felt like he'd been bashed against a rock. She turned her face from him. Without the sight of her, Collin felt like his world was in pieces.

"It's fine," she said.

It wasn't fine. He wasn't fine. Collin's chest was tight. His heart raced. His palms were sweaty.

"This won't really change our deal," Charlotte was saying. "You have access to your inheritance now. You'll be able to buy the horses at the auction. As for me, I'll start inquiring about a job at the Pemberley Races. I'm sure someone needs an assistant trainer or ranch hand."

"You're my ranch hand." That wasn't the right job. It wasn't the right position. Collin didn't want Charlotte as his ranch hand. "You're my partner."

"I can't stay on the ranch with you. Not with how I feel about you. It wouldn't be good for me."

She was frowning again. It was making Collin's chest ache to see it. He wracked his brain, trying to determine how he could make her smile again.

"I'm going to look for a job out of town. I think it's time for me to find a place where I belong."

You belong with me. That's what Collin wanted to say. That's what he should've said. But he felt it would make her even more sad.

He didn't want to make Charlotte sad. He

couldn't figure out how to make her happy. He didn't know how to fix this. And she was already pulling away from him.

"This will be for the best," she was saying as she stepped away. "You're getting what you've always wanted, and I'm happy I could help with that."

She wasn't happy. She was sad. And she was wrong.

This wasn't what Collin wanted. If Charlotte left town, he wouldn't get to see her face any longer. He wouldn't get to warm her hands. He wouldn't get to kiss her lips.

She was already gone from the room. Beyond his reach. Her absence left him feeling empty.

A hand clapped down on his back. It was Fitz. Collin sensed the touch was meant to be comforting. The gesture shocked Collin because the two of them weren't prone to outward displays of affection. Collin didn't want to hug his cousin. He wanted to hold his wife.

"What happened?" asked Carlos.

"She said she loves me," said Collin.

"Did you tell her you love her back?" said Carlos.

"I..." Collin scratched at his chest. There was an ache in his heart. Which was preposterous.

Heartache was a made-up thing. Heartburn was real, but he didn't like spicy foods.

His head felt dizzy. He wanted to lie down and sob. When he told this to the guys, Carlos punched him on the shoulder.

"That's love, you idiot," said Carlos.

"Is that how I fix this?" Collin asked. "Do I go back and tell her I feel sick?"

"I don't think that would be very romantic," said Fitz.

"What do I do? I don't want to lose her. She thinks I got everything I wanted out of our deal. I'll give back the inheritance and all the horses if she would just come back to me."

"Perfect," said Carlos. "Then that's what you'll do."

CHAPTER TWENTY-THREE

"Thank you. It was very nice to meet you. I'll follow up with you next week."

Charlotte had said those words to a number of ranchers and trainers she'd met at the auction. Most were impressed with her credentials. Not enough to make her a head trainer, but enough to consider bringing her on as an assistant or a hand.

Funny how there was opportunity when she put herself out there and didn't just wait and hope for someone to pick her.

She had a handful of business cards and a list of owners to email for follow-ups. Still, none of the jobs made her excited. No one else was doing the work that Collin was doing in saving retired or injured racehorses. They were all more interested in the latest tactics and techniques to make their prized horses faster.

Charlotte looked down the stalls at the horses up for auction. Many of them looked weary and tired. There was no excitement in their eyes about the rest of their lives. Because the rest of their lives were uncertain.

They weren't guaranteed to get a kind hand, or a roof over their heads, or food in their belly. Not unless they struck Collin Hunsford's fancy. Each of these horses would be lucky to be chosen to go to Rosings Ranch.

Charlotte envied every one of them. There was a part of her that wanted to go to Rosings Ranch. There was a part of her that wanted to sit by and hope for Collin to pick her.

He'd already done that. Twice, now. And the last time, she'd walked away from him. She knew she wouldn't be so lucky a third time.

"Charlotte?"

"Collin." Charlotte turned to the sound of that deep voice. Unfortunately, it wasn't Collin. It was his cousin. "Oh, hello, Fitz."

"How are you doing today?"

"Me? I'm fine. Just fine."

Those eyes, so much like Collin's, pierced into

Charlotte. It saw the lie. It waited patiently for the truth.

"I will be fine," she conceded. "Is he here?"

"Yes. He asked me to give this to you."

Fitz handed Charlotte an auction paddle. These were only given out to the owners, who were prepared to make a bid on the horses up for sale. Charlotte stared at the instrument as though it was a foreign object.

"What's it for?" she said.

"He wants you to bid on a lot you think is worthy."

Before Charlotte could ask another question, Fitz tipped his cowboy hat and melded into the crowd. Charlotte looked out over a sea of cowboy hats. She knew she could've found Fitz Darcy. The man towered above the heads of others, and he had an unmistakable gait to his walk. One that set him apart from everyone else.

She didn't trail behind him to ask more questions about Collin. She held the paddle, cradling it to her heart. It was her only connection to him.

Collin still trusted her judgment on horses. That was something. Something she could hold on to. Even if it would be the last tie between them.

Charlotte made her way to the seating area. Eliza

and Jane were seated with their father. They'd saved her a seat.

"You're bidding?" asked Eliza.

"Collin left it for me."

"You spoke to him?"

"No, Fitz gave it to me."

"Darcy? What's he up to." Eliza glared around the sea of cowboy hats, but Fitz was no longer within sight. "I don't see Collin anywhere, and they're about to begin."

Charlotte had been looking around for him, too. She hadn't caught a single sign of him. But she knew he was near. She felt his presence. She hungered for one more glimpse of him, even knowing what it would do to her heart.

"First item on the lot is a bit unusual," said the announcer. "Starting with the fact that this stallion has two legs and not four."

The curtains opened to reveal... a man. The audience keeled over with raucous laughter. Charlotte sat up straight when she saw Collin standing on stage.

He looked uncomfortable. Like the laughter was eating away at him. But he held himself straight, proud, and tall. What was he doing up there?

"This is a young man," the announcer continued.

"As you can see, he's in his prime. Though it says here that he suffers from a fractured heart muscle. Unlike most stallions, he is the kind to mate for life. But he's lost his mate."

There were a few feminine ahhhs mixed in with the masculine laughter.

"He has good stable manners. Though he needs more training to recognize human cues, especially from women. He does understand and responds to smiles."

Now the ahhs were overtaking the chuckles.

"Also," the announcer peered intently at the card he read from, "he is fine with being tied up."

Collin winced and looked over to the side of the stage where Carlos Bingley stood grinning broadly. Carlos made a twirling motion with his fingers. Collin shook his head, a clear refusal to show the crowd what he was working with from all sides.

"He is looking for a female trainer who can love him and be patient with him as he endeavors to show that he can love her back. We will start the bidding now."

Charlotte's hands were shaking. So much so that the auction paddle, the paddle he'd sent to her, slipped from her hands. Thankfully, her best friend was there to come to her rescue.

Eliza grabbed the paddle and raised it high in the air. Collin's gaze latched onto the paddle. When he saw its holder, he cringed. Eliza took Charlotte's hand and stuffed the stick in her palm. Then Charlotte's best friend glared down at anyone who dared to raise their own paddle.

And so it was with the help of her best friend that Charlotte won herself a prized stallion. Charlotte had no idea how much she paid for the lot. But she would not complain. She would never complain, not with that open display of affection.

Never in her wildest dreams would she have imagined that Collin would make such a spectacle of himself. Out in front of the whole town. All to show her what she meant to him.

It was beyond what Charlotte had hoped for. She couldn't wait for the end of the auction. She hopped up out of her seat and met her stallion at the edge of the stage.

"It didn't work," said Collin. "You're still crying."

Charlotte shook her head. "Ask me what kind of tears these are."

Collin cupped her cheek, catching a couple of tears before they fell. "I hope they're happy tears."

Charlotte nodded.

Collin wrapped his other arm around her and

pulled her close. "I do love you, Charlotte. You make my heart speed up. You make my head foggy. My stomach grumbles like I'm going to be sick. But then, when I hold you in my arms, the rest of the world falls away, and all I see is your smile."

Charlotte's heart raced in tune to his. Her stomach was doing belly flips of its own. But her head was clear. All she could see was the man she loved with her whole heart and mind.

"I want you to be my wife, and my friend, and my partner."

Charlotte let go of all the business cards in her hand. She'd found the job of her dreams, all being offered to her by the man of her dreams. "I want that, too."

"You're smiling." Collin breathed a sigh of relief. "It's a true smile. It touches your eyes."

It touched her eyes, her heart, her soul. Charlotte lifted her face to Collin's until she met his lips. Collin was smiling, too. She covered his smile with hers and felt like she would drown in happiness.

As they deepened the kiss, she distantly heard the sound of people whooping and clapping. A few horses neighed in the background as well. That's what brought her back around.

"Okay," Charlotte said, pulling away. "Now it's time to get down to business."

Collin looked at her, confused. The desire was palpable in his eyes. There would be plenty of time for that. They had to be sensible first.

"You're not the only horse I plan to have in my stable," said Charlotte.

Collin grinned as he reached for her hand with the paddle. He put his arm around her as they took their seats and began bidding for the future they planned to have together.

EPILOGUE

"When are you flying back out here?"

Carlos shrugged. When he realized that his publicist couldn't see the noncommittal motion, he used his words. "I don't know, Caroline. I told you I need a break."

"You're hot right now, Carlos. We need to keep the interest going."

Carlos's interest was currently focused across the ranch. Jane Bennett held her friend Charlotte's left hand in hers. Jane's smile was broad and bright as she gushed over Charlotte's wedding ring. Carlos couldn't see the diamond sparkling from here. What he did see was the sparkle in Jane's green eyes.

"Carlos? Are you listening to me?"

Carlos had not been listening. He gave his head, but in his mind's eye, he still held fast to Jane's sparkle. It was inside him now. Just like he had gotten inside him the first time he'd seen her years ago.

"If you want Hollywood to come calling," Caroline was saying, "then you need to be here, being seen around Hollywood."

That was just the point. Carlos wasn't sure if he wanted Hollywood to come calling. He wasn't even sure if he wanted to head back down to Mexico to sign a new contract to star in a highly anticipated Telenovela.

The first time he'd stepped onto a stage and into a role, it was for fun. He'd joined the theater program in high school because Jane was volunteering in the costume department. Carlos was all thumbs when it came to needle and thread, but he'd assumed if she had to take his measurements, then he'd have a reason to talk to her.

He'd been shocked when he was offered the lead role in the school play that year. His costume had been special-ordered so he hadn't had much cause to talk to Jane who'd been tasked with making the extras' costumes. After opening night, an agent who'd been in town to visit a friend of a friend had spotted Carlos. It was a blur after that which had him pulled out of school and landed on a set in Mexico where he'd starred in three long-running series.

And now he was back.

Carlos's gaze found Jane again. He hadn't lied to Caroline. He did need a break. He was about to take a shot at the biggest break of his life.

"You need to date."

Carlos blinked back to the phone conversation he'd been ignoring. Finally, he and Caroline were on the same page. "Yeah, I think you might be right about that."

"I have a few women auditioning for the role of your girlfriend as we speak."

That was the other thing about acting. Every supporting role in his life since he'd gotten top billing was meticulously cast. Each of his girlfriends over the last ten years, including the first date he'd ever been on, even his first kiss, had been fake. He'd never had a real date. Never had a real girlfriend. There were times he wasn't sure if his friends were real.

That's why he'd come home to Austen Valley.

Darcy was a real friend. Carlos even enjoyed Collin's company. Neither man suffered any fools.

Jane had offered her friendship. He'd starred in enough melodramas with this plotline to know he had a shot. He'd been nominated for an Emmy for his skills. Maybe he had the chops to turn their friendship into something more?

"What if I'm already dating someone?" he said into the receiver.

"Like for real? No, no. That won't do."

"Why not?"

"Because you can't date a real girl. Who would even believe that? It would look fake. I'll book you on a flight for tonight. You'll be dating a reality star by the weekend."

"I'm not flying out tonight."

"When then?"

"Not for a few more weeks. I have some unfinished business here."

Caroline continued to squawk and protest into the phone. Carlos hit the end button. Then he took a step towards Jane Bennett aiming to finish what he'd started all those years ago.

See if Carlos can deliver the right line to make Jane his
leading lady in
"a Truth Universally Acknowledged"
Book Two of the Pemberley Ranch Romances!

Shanae Johnson was raised by Saturday Morning cartoons and After School Specials. She still doesn't understand why there isn't a life lesson that ties the issues of the day together just before bedtime. While she's still waiting for the meaning of it all, she writes stories to try and figure it all out. Her books are wholesome and sweet, but her are heroes are hot and heroines are full of sass!

And by the way, the E elongates the A. So it's pronounced Shan-aaaaaaaa. Perfect for a hero to call out across the moors, or up to a balcony, or to blare outside her window on a boombox. If you hear him calling her name, please send him her way!

You can sign up for Shanae's Reader Group at http://bit.ly/ShanaeJohnsonReaders

Also By Shanae Johnson

The Pemberley Ranch Romances

In Want of a Wife

a Truth Universally Acknowledged

In Possession of a Good Fortune

How Ardently I Love You

The Brides of Purple Heart

On His Bended Knee

Hand Over His Heart

Offering His Arm

His Permanent Scar

Having His Back

In Over His Head

Always On His Mind

Every Step He Takes

In His Good Hands

Light Up His Life

Strength to Stand

The Rangers of Purple Heart

The Rancher takes his Convenient Bride

The Rancher takes his Best Friend's Sister

The Rancher takes his Runaway Bride

The Rancher takes his Star Crossed Love

The Rancher takes his Love at First Sight

The Rancher takes his Last Chance at Love

The Silver Star Ranch Romances

His Pledge to Honor

His Pledge to Cherish

His Pledge to Protect

His Pledge to Have

His Pledge to Hold

The Flying Cross Ranch Romances

His Vow to Love

His Vow to Trust

His Vow to Treasure

His Vow to Adore

His Vow to Respect

His Vow to Defend

RETURN TO DUBLIN, TN:

Everyday Heroes

By

IRENE E. BECKER

RETURN TO DUBLIN, TN: EVERYDAY HEROES